The Singing

Stephanie Bishop

16
EasyRead Large

Copyright Page from the Original Book

First published in 2005
by Brandl & Schlesinger Pty Ltd
PO Box 127 Blackheath NSW 2785 Australia
www.brandl.com.au

This project has been assisted by the Commonwealth Government
through the Australia Council, its arts funding and advisory body.

 This book was published with the generous help of
Varuna – The Writers' House, Katoomba.

National Library of Australia Cataloguing-in-Publication entry:

Bishop, Stephanie, 1979-.
The singing.
ISBN 1 876040 54 8
1. Man-woman relationships – Fiction. I. Title.
A823.4

Cover and book designed by András Berkes

Set in 11 pt Garamond

Printed in Australia by Griffin Press

Stephanie Bishop

The Singing

Stephanie Bishop was born in Sydney in 1979. The recipient of several writer's fellowships, including a Varuna Mentorship Fellowship, her work has been published in various literary journals and anthologies throughout Australia. She will shortly be commencing her PhD at the University of Cambridge in the Department of English and is working on her second novel.

For Alice M.

The Public would say that a novel devoted to influenza lacked plot; they would complain that there was no love in it – wrongly however for illness often takes on the guise of love, and plays the same old tricks.

Virginia Woolf, *On Being Ill*

Introducing The Singing

Peter Bishop
Creative Director, Varuna – The Writers' House

For some reason, most new works are presented to the public without introduction. A new edition of a classic might merit an introduction, a careful placing in a literary or historical context. But a new work is assumed to belong clearly to its time and to need no placing within this time.

Reading a Jean Rhys novel recently, I enjoyed the thoughtful, well-researched introduction, and remembered that Jean Rhys's first book of stories, *The Left Bank,* had in fact been presented to the world under the patronage of a long, grandiose and opinionated introduction by Ford Madox Ford. Ford's final paragraph – and he has been talking for more than ten pages – unwittingly gives a very good reason why a new writer should perhaps be allowed to appear on stage unmolested by introduction:

"One likes [writes Ford], in short, to be connected with something good, and Miss Rhys's work seems to me to be so very good, so vivid, so extraordinarily distinguished by the rendering of passion, and so true, that I wish to be connected with it. I hope I shall bring her a few readers and so when – hundreds of years hence! – her ashes are translated to the Panthéon, in the voluminous pall, the cords of which are held by the most prominent of the Haute Bourgeoisie of France, a grain or so of my scattered and forgotten dust may go in too, in the folds."

Jean Rhys's own dry and excellent reply to such windiness is found in the unsparing portrait of her patron in her first novel, *Quartet.*

So with some diffidence I introduce Stephanie Bishop's first novel, *The Singing.* I remember the moment when Stephanie told me the title she had chosen. There had been other titles, but this was a title that immediately and mysteriously described the whole being of this strange and captivating novel. Other titles spoke of what the novel was about: *The Singing* is what the novel is.

I have found myself thinking a lot about the composer Sibelius. After bringing audiences to their feet in his first three symphonies, what might he have expected an audience to make of the quiet winter light and bleak storm landscape of the fourth symphony? To a friend he wrote that the new symphony would have "nothing, absolutely nothing, of the circus about it". To his publisher, who might well have expressed disappointment or even dismay at the unfriendly new symphony, he said: "Other composers bring you cocktails; I bring only spring water." For the critic Rosa Newmarch the symphony was the composer "alone with nature breathing things".

The Singing is not a work of circuses and cocktails. It is a work of spring water, solitude, quietness, breathing. Within that breathing, within the singing, there is intense drama.

Listen to it.

> The world has ended,
> I must carry you.

Paul Celan, *Grosse, Glühende Wölbung*

Not long ago a man approached me on the street. He said he had caught sight of me from a distance and had followed, catching up at the lights two blocks ahead. He said he thought it was me, but couldn't be certain, having seen only the back of my head, and had had trouble, because I looked so different, was wearing such different clothes – a skirt, shoes instead of boots. I was what my mother would call well groomed. You look beautiful, he said, more so than I remember. Taller, and – rounder, your face is rounder – it is the shape of your mother's after all, as you told me, not your father's.

You never knew my father, I said.

There were pictures, you showed me pictures.

I did not know what to say to this. I had shown him everything. And it had been so many years since we had spoken. He was wondering if I had children, his eyes flickered to my hand, looking, I think, for a ring. He should know though, that I never wanted that sort of thing.

We were on George Street. There was traffic and people pushing past. I could see him continuing to speak but could not hear him, his voice falling beneath the engines of buses, trucks.

He was thinner than I remembered. I think he was wearing the same kind of suit. It was the same colour, dark although not quite black. I refused lunch – although I realise now that he had only suggested coffee. I was really quite busy, I said. Yes, of course. As he walked away then I recognised again the rise of his shoulder blade beneath his shirt, the bone that, clipped, like a wing, I could lift and dig my thumb beneath.

He is all that holds me to what I once was. And between us there are large spaces, vague, refusing to be filled. Where, when, I was not one thing or another, neither sick nor well, when I told him that in order for me to find which I had most become I would have to leave.

You look well, he had said. No – the word was beautiful. You look beautiful. And I was struck then by what I must have been before. Narrow, weak, aged already.

He sees me now and I am young again, despite the sense that I will, as a consequence, always be old.

I consider the future now as much as I consider the past. Time is not linear; no, I see it differently. Time hums and does not drive like a car does. This is how I come across it: bunched in inaccessible shadows or running clean. And there are moments when every instant of time past hovers close together and pushes itself towards the future, making the fate of things appear to us. Like meeting him on the street, a moment when I sensed, as though in water, the coming warm and cool pockets of time's sorrow and relief.

Illness makes the past not the past. It makes it always present. And erased, some of it, time and the time that has gone inside it. And how hard – and how unfruitfully – one can try to rediscover it once its disappearance has been realised. So when I saw him on the street he must have known – that so much of me is a disguise, the way we all think we are all disguised.

He knows, I think, of my double life, straddling two worlds, two fears – of love, of not love. But it is not only a double life that I lead: it is a triple, quadruple, infinite life made up of the moments and years of relations, past and future, that I live between. And there is no way, however hard I try, to hold them all.

Standing there on the corner of the street we were not far from where we used to walk, early on, by the water. And it was cold again; it had always been cold here, tall buildings channelling the wind. But sunny, by the harbour it had always been sunny. In fact it had always been unbearably bright.

We would walk around the water, that thick dark water, walking between all that concrete. It was a blank place except for our voices. There were seagulls, pigeons – Paris pigeons, you said – and people jogging in their lunch break, a woman paddling her feet in the grimy water. We would be distracted by these things, caught up in conversation, so that often the tourist trams driving up behind us had to sound their horns. I recall that it was often you telling me to move, gently. I remember the first time you touched your hand to my back to shift me out of the way. It was glary. The cement reflected the light. I was squinting and the yellow and white of the tram blurred in the brightness.

You had glasses on. Dark sunglasses that made it difficult to see your eyes and I found myself disconcerted, speaking towards my own reflection.

When we met again on the street and parted, he reached out a hand to touch me, on the arm, just beneath my elbow, smiling as though his heart were behind his eyes. His warmth reminding me of my coldness, and how I thought I had lost it, sloughed it off. You are mistaken, I wanted to say, I am not that any more.

But I know he knows. I know he knows my brittleness, and that it is only fear, all fear. Even speaking to him like that on the street. And he was still so charming, his face had hardly changed, so soft, and I hoped, although I did not ask, that there was someone else who loved it now. But I don't know this. In fact I do not think I want to know – if it is someone delightful, someone well, the effervescent woman of my past that I gave up on. Someone young.

I am imagining. I am always imagining. His life, like the one he might imagine for me, is probably none of these things.

I am sorry, I wanted to say, I am sorry, but for what I am not sure.

It is I, then, who sees him from behind, crossing the street, walking away. He did not say to where.

To a short-sighted person someone in the distance can blur at the edges, so they appear as if encircled by a bright halo. This becomes particularly apparent if one looks for a long time without blinking, as I did, watching him shrink in the distance of the street.

It was as though we had been collected by a hand of fate. We were one another's underworld and we could have led one another out. Yet we failed, and I cannot understand exactly how that meeting, on the street, ended the way it did. Was it I, Orpheus like, who looked back to you and caused your descent into the city street, to be lost forever. Or was it you who did not turn back, who never did turn back (but was that for the love of something?), and I, Eurydice, who refused to follow.

***

It becomes hard to experience what separateness is when you are in such proximity, and yet without it one cannot know what one is seeing. Yet it is impossible to see nothing, for even with the eyes closed or in complete darkness the mind will invent something to see: shadows, lights, things flickering. Seeing what is not before us and failing to see what is. It is hard work, I know now, to try to turn someone into a stranger; to try to make a man disappear.

Send me away, he whispered once. Send me away. It was night; he thought I was sleeping, that I could not hear. But I could not do that then. And now I find I have without intending.

I did not say to him anything that I meant.

I wanted to say that I can explain everything.

I no longer lived in the city on the day that I saw him. I had not lived there for years. He knew this. In the year after my sickness I recovered sufficiently to work again and decided to travel. My work took me away and I have spent much time since moving between places and writing, as I do now, from hotel rooms.

He asked me where I was staying and I told him. He looked a little surprised, it is an expensive hotel and he was not aware that my work had made me so successful. But in the beginning, when I was well, he had always said that he had great hopes for me, that he always suspected I would go far. I was staying quite close to where we stood, in fact in a hotel overlooking the harbour which we had once walked past and said to each other that we should go there for a weekend, although we never did. I told him he was more than welcome to come and see me there, and that I would be in the city for two weeks. Thank you, he said, he might. Do, I said, it would be lovely to see you. Yes, he replied.

I thought perhaps he might come. I hoped that he would, but I expected he would not. I told myself that I should expect him not to although my hope was that he would. I gave him my room number and he wrote it down on a slip of paper and above it he wrote my name. I was upset by this. He should not need my name there. And were he to lose the number he need only come to the front desk and ask for me and the woman there would call me and tell me that there was a man here to see me and I would know who it was without needing his name and I would come downstairs and see him and be surprised. I would act as if I had not been thinking of him, sitting here in my room and writing about him. What a surprise, I would say, I'm so glad you came. It is, as I must have said on the street, so lovely to see you. And if I were not in my room at the time the woman at the desk would tell him this and would ask him if he would like to leave a message. I imagine that he would leave just his name, or not even that, saying only to tell me that he had called; I, he would say, just let her know that I called, assuming that there was no one else who would call on me. He would not call again. If he decided to visit it would be on a whim. So he would say – he would say that he just happened to be passing. He would lie; at least I would hope that if he made our meeting out to be such a casual thing that it would be because he was lying.

She walked quickly through the house, down the stairs from the bedroom and along the corridor. She knew what she had to do. She had her green woollen coat on and her boots. She was going to leave a note. She did try. She moved her hands over the surface of the desk but could not find the paper. You can turn the light on, he had said. He was awake. No, I don't need it, she said, go to sleep. Come back to bed, he said. Yes, she replied, in a minute.

She passed through the living room, past the fire that he would collect wood for and light in the morning, and above it the mantelpiece with the blue vase holding yellow and white chrysanthemums. He said he had thought all day about what flowers to buy her. She had never decided on her favourites. All day? Yes. He chose bright ones. And long lasting. She glanced at them, and at the postcard leaning against the vase. It was of a cathedral in Europe that her mother had visited. She wrote of angels and of a bad restaurant in Venice. There were dogs allowed. Dogs.

She reached the front door. She opened it. It was a dark night. The sky had been grey for days. She should have worn a scarf. Too late now, she would wake him again and instead went out through the garden, past the lavender and the weeds and towards the road that would lead her to the lake and then the highway.

It is no good, she had said, you are all goodness.

Yes. That is what everyone has always said. He was upset by this. He could hate his own kindness.

Forgive me. There is no one who could have done more than you.

There were puddles at the roadside. The white streetlights were reflected in them and she could hear a party going on across the valley. There were bright lights through the trees and music. Someone was singing. A birthday. The people in the house with the garden full of roses perhaps, over near the church and the park with the fir tree decorated all year round for Christmas.

She kept going. Her foot caught on a stone and she stumbled. Her fists were clenched. It was cold – there will be frost soon, he had said. The highway was further than she thought, even the lake with its pale wooden pylons and its geese seemed such a long way, and although she had not gone far she was, as always, tired already. Come to me, come to me, he'd say and hold her head in his hands, one on her forehead one behind, but he was not here, she thought, passing the old man walking his dog. She had seen him often. It was all he did – in his brown vest, his hat and gloves. He nodded to her and called the dog towards him, a tennis ball in his hand. Sally, he called, Sal. With love. But she did not envy him. He had probably already lost everything, she thought. And it is just the two of them left, just the two of them.

She was growing dizzy. Again. She could not focus on the road. Her head had started its chattering, her mind ringing sharply in her ears as the wind whipped at her cheeks and her bare hands and threw the dry leaves up beneath the streetlights. Above her it whinnied in the trees. A car came and she stepped to the side of the road where the headlights would not catch her while the leaves skidded about in front of it. There were more leaves with another gust of wind and another and the car drove over them, she could hear them. Their thin dry bodies breaking beneath the tyres. Red and star-shaped from the maple tree. A dog barked. You are always hearing things, he said. Like an animal. What do dogs bark at? Wind. Wind in the trees. The gums shaking their branches like the halftime entertainment girls fisting pom poms at a football game.

Take it, he had said. Take everything.

She thought of this but she could not go any further. She knew she would never reach the water or the highway. She turned around. The shadows were dark beneath the trees. They were cold, they felt like water in her mouth and her hands moved away from her in search of home. At the edge of the road she took hold of the fence and followed its cold metal that ran down the side of the garden and along the back. Some distance ahead a darker shape appeared, taking further form as she approached. It was the woman in the house opposite, crying in her garden. She knows this woman, the smell of lavender, the summer dress over a pair of men's trousers. She had said once, pointing upwards, look, the sky has a tear in it. It had been the sun coming out. And pointing to a cloud she had said be careful of the puddles. Then she had whistled, sharp and clear like a man would whistle before quickly withdrawing inside her house.

There appeared a shape then, in the verandah light of her own house. He called out a name. Is that you? he said.

There was no fence to separate the house from the road, just a stretch of dry grass and some low bushes marking an official boundary. A drive overgrown with weeds ran to one side and then there was a tree, beside it a bird bath that never held water. She could see the woman from where she stood, clutching at the fence by the roadside. She could see her sitting on the ground near the tree.

She saw the open door of her house. A light on, a man in tree shadow. He smells of sleep. He has said that even when she is awake she smells of sleep. What is that smell? Warm, he said.

You'll catch cold. His hands are out, he is walking across the yard. You'll wake people, he says, as a light comes on in the house next door and then another. They have red curtains. They open them.

Come on, he says. She is holding the fence with one hand and the night with the other and she can still see the woman crying and every time she has seen her the woman has said they have gone now. Sad, isn't it, they have gone now. And she wants to know who, who it is that has left.

He is behind her now. His hands are on her shoulders, and the house, she can see the house, the inside of it suddenly all around her. And the light is all around her and her mouth is pushed against his red shirt, and she can feel his hands come, holding her head, his hands held over her ears like shells, and he says Ssh, he says, Ssh, Ssh. Here, listen to the ocean, and she can hear it and she can hear it.

Beside him she fell asleep. She woke once more, later into the night, to reach for the glass of water on the windowsill, her figure appearing dark and thin in the room where he now lay awake. She had come up against him and he could feel the small hairs of her back on his stomach. It had been like this before, but differently, when they had lived in the terrace in the city. She would keep him awake then too. Talking. Both of them too tired to sleep, after having danced for hours. At least she danced. He had tried but was awkward, although she didn't mind this, she'd laugh. He'd laugh. He liked her laughing. The hugeness of it, how he could not hear her over the music and could see just her face, laughing soundlessly in the dark.

The morning would be coming soon. He got up and moved towards his clothes that lay crumpled on the floor. He picked up his jacket and his shoes and carried them out of the room so as not to disturb her. It would be cold outside. It was July and winter had set in.

It was in the winter of – I have forgotten. I could count back according to my age and find the date when the middle of our things began, if middles begin, but it does not matter. We had begun. It was winter. Besides, memory is the same as history: and they are both like giving. Shaped by the things that are withheld as much as by the things that are offered. Time is used as a witness. It says, this and this happened inside me. It was winter. We had begun.

Take it, he had said. Take everything. But he did not mean me and all my things. He meant him.

I did not go, that night when I set out to. It was not a failure. It had never been a plan. Escape just happens. Or doesn't. We have relapses with many things; mine was him.

I could hear his boots below, in the kitchen. Then I heard him on the stairs. He had been out early collecting firewood and came in quietly, opening the door just an inch to see if I had woken. You're up, he said, I have brought you an orange. He came in, sat on the edge of the bed and began to peel it, his thumb digging into the skin and taking it back. It came off in thick pieces. As it broke a fine spray tore into the air. He worked slowly and I could hear the skin as it ripped away from the fruit.

He collected the peel in his lap and broke the orange into pieces. It made a softer sound as each segment was tugged from the one next to it. I watched carefully. His eyes met mine for a moment and returned to the fruit. He smelled faintly of fuel from the chainsaw and of the cold. I could feel it coming off his body. And of oranges, he smelled of oranges. It was finished then. He passed me a piece and took some for himself.

Can you peel it again?

I just did.

The pith.

He took the piece back. The whole room smelt of oranges.

There, he said, passing it to me as he pushed my hair back from my face.

He watched her, every moment housed by memory. He could not see her and not consider the past. Even if it didn't come to words, if it emerged instead as a splinter of a picture or as sorrow. It came in strange things, often in thoughts of her dancing – dancing, she'd say, until she was animal – or of her speech, rapid and witty and always too loud. He used to have to remind her in public places to quieten – in the library, in art galleries especially – but she would only laugh.

What came on and pervaded her, changing her indelibly, came on slowly and worked its way through – not in, for it seemed as though it did not come from outside, not from the air, but instead from some point of contact, from the ground, from some object that she had touched. As if whatever it was were given a moment of reception then lay in waiting, appearing at first as a symptom of so many things. For anything once lost or disliked. Her job perhaps, the noise of the city. As if presenting in some solid form a resistance, a recent sorrow. But that made no sense, there had not been before it anything great enough. It could have been explained, he had thought at first, by the nights of wakefulness, of talk, but it had a different form, a different texture, it was weighted and damp and did not lift even after sleep.

It is a strange thing to think (he thought, she thought) that illness might be considered to occur when some connection is lost, with a person or a place; that malaise might arise out of grief. Out of an absence or a void, from a discrepancy too great to comprehend, like some great passion or temper that exceeds any boundary of the body, and that refuses the limits that might be suggested by another. These things that overflow notions of capacity and common sense.

But there was no one moment when it could be said that my illness, as such, began, and it should be explained that this term, *illness,* was arrived at for want of a better one. It was for the sake of simplicity, for the matter of identification and the need for relationship. I have been told that there was a philosopher who said 'I have given a name to my pain and I call it dog', and I understood such a necessary but insufficient definition of suffering quite completely.

After my orange he helped me move downstairs. I was on the lounge with the blue Persian rug at my feet and he was walking from the kitchen through the living room and towards the front door. It was a beautiful day, he said. We should do something with it, opening the door as the day came towards us. He was eating half a piece of toast with marmalade and sipping a cup of black coffee.

Outside there was, as he had said, the day. The thin white bodies of trees stood still with their leaves to the sun; cabbage white butterflies – he pointed to them – just new today, in this new type of day; the frayed nerve of it, the light bittered yet still full of hope. I could see it shining on the gloss of the windowsill. I could see it on the glass, and inside the glass that rested on the table.

There had been water in the glass. This was somehow frightening, the light in the glass that had held water. Or maybe it was the glass itself that frightened me. He turned back from the door then and said the flowers on the mantelpiece are dead and I really should throw them out, I meaning me, but I liked them. I liked their composition and the way they continued to change, the green of them fading into yellow. I explained this while he watched the day from the window and said something about the air, how it was the air; the way its warmth came to us without warning, and found us, now, in a pistoned day shafted by a clean brightness. It was – we said it almost together – the perfect day for a picnic, the way the cold had turned warm so unexpectedly. He was standing beside me then, touching my arm in that automatic gesture of togetherness. I put my hand up to reach him.

The year passed like this, full of sudden unexpectedness, in likeness to the way we understood my condition. It was winter and we were given a strange warm day.

Over there, he said.

Where?

Over there – a child across the street is singing.

There have been times since then when I have called others by your name. Or I have thought, felt, your name and do not know what it was that I called them. What does it mean to bring you back like this, pursuing you in my memory and thinking of you in the same manner that I looked out for you long after you had turned away from me in the street?

People often talk of living with the wounds and divisions of war within the one body and this thought clings to me, bothers me, because I believe it but do not want to limit division to that. For it seems that we commit violence and hold suffering in so many ways and I will live divided by you and illness always.

I returned to my hotel room after seeing you. I had only arrived in the city that morning and had gone out for a walk to restore myself, having travelled all night. But you exhausted me still, and instead of walking any further I went back. I unlocked my door, lay down on the bed and tried to sleep.

I had just drifted off when there was a knock at the door. It was not you. It was the man from concierge with my bags. He knocked at the door and I delayed opening it a moment, unsure as to whether or not I had dreamed the knock. There it was again though and again and I opened the door. I looked at the bags a moment. I did not recognise them. He had said, Your luggage, madam, holding in one hand a pink dress on a coat hanger and in the other a dark green shoulder bag. I did not recognise either of them. I looked at them, holding the door open, and the man stood there, telling me that these were my belongings and I thought for a moment that if he said so then perhaps they must be, but they were not.

These are not my belongings, I said to him. They are not? he said. No. He froze a moment; he had made a mistake. Oh, he said, yours are the two small black cases. Yes. I will be right back, he said. Thank you, I replied and closed the door.

I lay back down on the bed. The sun streamed in through the window, a terribly bright, terribly white light, and from my small but expensive room I had a view of rooftops. I closed my eyes. There was another knock at the door. The concierge man. I got up. He had my bags. Your luggage, he reported. Thank you, I said and he carried it into the room while I held the door open. There was nothing in there to see but he made a point of not looking around, casting only one furtive glance as he put my bags down and turned back towards the door. Then he was outside the room in the corridor. Thank you, I said again. He was clearly embarrassed about the previous mistake and must have run down the stairs and back up again for I noticed that there was sweat above his top lip and that his face was flushed. He was a handsome man. He was not a man, it seemed, who would make mistakes often. And this was an expensive hotel, one expected the right luggage. As he left I thanked him again and he almost whispered, he did whisper, or perhaps it was just breathlessness, but whatever the case, it was strange, for he said to me, take care, as though I were known to him.

I unpacked my clothes, showered and put on a fresh shirt. It was only five in the evening but I was hungry so I went out to eat.

As I began to walk it started raining. It came on heavily and unexpectedly and the whole city opened its umbrellas. Men appeared suddenly at street corners and called out *um-ber-ell-a, um-ber-ell-a*. No thank you. No thank you. They were there for the unprepared. I had seen the clouds though and, as always, had packed an umbrella.

I made my way through the streets towards a restaurant I had passed in the morning. Ahead I could see its glass doors opening onto the wet pavement and I went in. It was empty; all the tables set with cutlery and plastic flowers in small white vases. I took a seat at a table for two and a French man served me. He offered me the refreshments menu although I wanted dinner, and said that they did not begin serving the evening meal until six. It was five-thirty. I did not understand why they could not feed me what I wanted, seeing as I was the only customer present, but he assured me that I could not have dinner until six. I order a drink and wait.

I am in his part of town now. I am not here thinking about him because I am pursuing him but I imagine that if I saw him again and he had not seen me that I would follow him. I think about him now because I am here and when I am here it is impossible not to think of him, and because it is raining. It is raining again. It is raining and despite my umbrella I am wet and uncomfortable and when I am uncomfortable and cold like this I think of him because he used always to comfort me, and I think of talking to him, the way we had of talking, and of him offering me dry clothes to wear. Because it is nice to have someone to care for.

But what would we do if we were to come across each other again in the street. What would we do. A friend said to me once that she thought you either loved someone or you did not. Boys, she said. When talking about men she always referred to them as boys. And in between, she went on, it is difficult, because you do not know – what you want, why you want it, what is good for you. But once you overstep that and you no longer love them it is very hard to come back. I am afraid of this. I am afraid, and have always been afraid of seeing him again because of this. Because it is nice to love. Because it is good, even if it is terrible, to have the hope that there is some great happiness waiting for you, if you can just get things right.

He wrote once, I think of you. I think of you, he said.

And what do we do now with this freedom. What is it that we do with freedom. Some days I cannot remember the colour of it.

For I imagine that he is, right now, in this city. Working, presumably, at the same nine-to-five job that would send me mad yet kept him sane, filing and typing on the fourth floor of a building in Pitt Street. He used to joke about the tie he wore around his neck and his work for the government, as though he were working for some secret service and had, within himself, the potential for corruption.

He was not an administrator by nature. He was not organised, did not think in the organised pattern that administrative work requires, although he was patient and very precise. Meticulous in fact; he cared for me meticulously. But if he had a nature it was as a painter. Of course, though, he knew that it would never earn him money and we had decided together that it was money we needed. A means to an end, he said. I was an expense.

Yet he was wearing his tie when I saw him. He was in the city. Clearly he had not returned to his painting as he had once promised me that he would. Not that I had ever doubted him or questioned his ability. We did our best to support one another. It was more, I realise now, that I must have warranted him with a greater ambition than he ever really had. He was not now what I had thought he would be. He seemed, somehow – less so, less happy. He could say though that he was none of these things, and had wanted none of these things. That I was the one who made him so. I had wanted so much for him. I had believed. But he was wearing a tie, he was not painting. No, he was just the same.

If his day runs as it did when I knew him then I know that he will soon be walking down this way, past this restaurant and towards the bar where he'll stop, as he always stopped, ordering a drink and smoking three cigarettes in succession. He will sit for half an hour by the window, watching the rain, and then drive home.

24

But he has already been and gone. Everywhere that I find myself I imagine that he has already been there and has just gone. While I remain, looking for a wet man in the street. A tall man in a dark suit. He never carried an umbrella. It depressed him, he said, to think ahead like that – to look at the sky and consider the possibility of rain. There was something very sad, he said, about carrying an umbrella around just in case.

I told him one night on the phone – I had already left by then and we spoke only that once, for hours though, well into the night – I told him, when we both said that we felt like we were dying, both in speaking to each other and in ending, that although I felt like I was dying, it didn't feel as though he was killing me. The pain, somehow, at the time, did not feel as though it was breaking me. It did not feel sharp like that because in many ways I had not gone at all, and, rather, had preserved him by my leaving. In this way, I presumed, ridiculously, that he would stay, that he would not walk away from me on the street. That he would not forget me. At the same time I wanted none of this. I say all of this now although I know, as he knows, that none of it is enough, that nothing is ever enough.

In the kitchen, I recall light fallen in a square on the floor, and outside, birds, and then just one, calling high low high low, the two sounds looping together and then, after listening, breaking apart into low low low with high between, two sounds disconnected from the one body, and I recall the trees, the one tree before the window, its lone branches reaching out, its fingers trembling. There you are, he'd say, coming to me, fixing the cushions, bringing me things, there you are, as though I had been lost and was now found.

Many years ago I worked in the city too and we would meet at the end of each day. It was late afternoon coming into evening on that day, one of those days near the beginning, and the sun setting across the harbour made the cold grey of the buildings look warm. I held onto him and we talked about insignificant things, the weather, the tedium of work and people, avoiding the other sorrow. But I said eventually, tell me – tell me about your sorrow. It sounds an overly romantic gesture I know, indulgent. But it was true. At that time that was all there was to say. He – who had left one woman, not for, but on the way had found, another. And I, whose sickness I suspect had already begun.

He was completely crippled at the time, burnt up. I thought of pigeon legs, those small red things dried and twisted beneath a body in flight and so I gave him a poem I had read. It was all I could do. He read it through in a café while I sat silently drinking tea. I wondered at the time what we looked like, and if we would ever look like that again – an old couple in company, engrossed in separate things. His Camel cigarettes on the table. My tea. The ribbing of his black sock and an inch of ankle. I have always had a peculiar weakness for men who smoke soft-packet cigarettes, and this being his first pack since he had quit seemed especially significant. It was a book, he said, it was the fault of a book that he had to start again. A fantastic story about a man who smoked and because the character smoked so well he could not help but start again himself.

He held a cigarette in one hand and the poem in the other. He read for a long time and then when he had finished leaned forward to put the cigarette out and said yes, still looking at the paper, that is how it was, although at the same time he said he did not feel a thing.

The world has always come in and out of focus. Now the world, now not the world. In the beginning, in fact in the very first week of their relationship, there was a complete absence of words to describe what it was they had embarked upon. It was less than a week, in the first twenty-four hours to be exact, that they realised this. It was the following morning, after they had spent the night together, when, lying there in his room in the city, half asleep with her head on his chest, the sun hitting the wooden floor beneath the closed curtains – that she asked him for words and he refused to give her any. He didn't want to name things, and although saddened by this, she knew that it was impossible to argue about a thing that had no name, and that it was even more impossible to argue with the person who refused to name the very thing that she was interested in arguing about; this thing between two people that remains nebulous even with the best of names and namers working on it, working nearly every minute of their lives in fact. Yet it remained as the foundation of their lives, even without a name, and how, she wanted to know, can a foundation be earthed if its very substance remains vacant?

With what could not be said about what they were becoming for one another hanging unresolved between them, they got up and went out to a café, she with a yellow bag over one shoulder and wearing his black jumper. They took a seat by a window that looked out onto a quiet street and ordered a pot of tea between them, their conversation starting up again around the nature of naming and nameless things, until, after pouring her a second cup, he put the teapot down and the tea strainer on the saucer beside it and, sitting back in his seat, looking at her or not looking at her she cannot remember which, said he thought their conversation, even the simple fact that they were having it, to be self-indulgent. He sipped his tea and put the cup down away from the saucer.

Why do you do that? she asked.

Do what?

That. Not use your saucer like that.

It annoyed him, he said, having to concentrate on where to put the cup down, when one should be able to put it down wherever one likes.

He made a joke then. She did not laugh. He had made a number of jokes through the course of the last twenty-four hours and she had not laughed. Why don't you ever laugh at my jokes? he asked.

Ever, she thought. Had there yet been an ever to do or not do anything in?

Well, she began. I don't find them funny.

He sipped his tea, and put the cup down again next to the saucer. She knew he thought that because she did not find his jokes funny that therefore she found nothing funny, and therefore was, ultimately, lacking a sense of humour completely. She said simply that she did not understand them, that she felt she existed on the other side of their more serious meaning. Besides, she said, you yourself do not find your own jokes funny, they are not funny, they are sad, and you make them because you are sad and you don't know what to do with your own sadness, and so you joke.

She looked around her. Although she knew they had only ordered tea, she felt certain that something else should arrive. She had a distinct sense of something not being there that should have been there. They had looked at the menu and considered gelato, but it seemed too cold and too early and after going through the motions of do you want it? I don't know, do you, I don't think so, but if you do – they decided no, neither of them felt like eating it. But even though there was nothing else to arrive, there remained that distinct feeling of something missing. Something that had been there and passed, like a meal, or their gelato, being ordered but then being carried straight past them and delivered to another table. That is ours! she would have exclaimed, standing to watch the misguided plate being shared by what appeared to be a couple identical to them.

The evening before, by the water, after he had finished his cigarette and the poem and had said, by way of saying that he did not feel a thing, that he could for some reason no longer feel things, we left the café we were in and crossed the bridge over the harbour. The wind rattled the flags on their poles and they billowed and flickered. Beyond them a large boat, a cruise ship, sounded its horn and a stream of brown smoke was released into the sky. It was a pale sky, dirty, and would have once been white, and before white, blue, were it not for the colour having been bleached out by the sun. I watched, waiting for the boat to move, slip away, leave land, and eventually it did, churning up the water behind it.

When I was five I waved my aunt off on a boat like that, I said. She was going on her honeymoon. I stood on the wharf with my mother and looked up; there were balloons and streamers, people blowing party horns and kisses. I'm sure I saw my aunt's face, and her new man, looking down at us and smiling and waving. But I imagine now that it could have been anyone, for there were so many people on that boat, all with their small windowless rooms below deck and the sun above. Tropical. They wanted things that were tropical. Exotic and sweet.

I could not see any colours on this boat though. I pointed this out to him. When we looked we could not even see any people. Although I imagined that they were there, I said, like ants, heading out to sea. He said nothing as we walked down the steps from the bridge and around the water, around that strange dead part of the city harbour. Tourists go there. And they walk like we do, did, drinking beer and eating ice-cream. They feed the seagulls and pigeons. Take photographs. We were a little like them. Passing through, trying to make sense of some strange place.

It must have been around seven when we took a table outside and ordered a drink. I had a gin, he bought it, while he drank beer. They gave me my drink in a small glass with a straw. I have never understood why they are served with a straw and as I squashed the slice of lemon up with it he said he had already done that for me.

It was a winter's day but it felt like spring, there was a warm wind, there were people with their tops off, in singlets, lying outside in the evening. And although I cannot describe either of us as actively pursuing the other, for we never took that leap, we never seemed that far apart, it was quite clear to me that I was, in some way, following him. His life was troubled at the time and he was a stranger to me in his sorrow. I say that, and say also that we were close. We were both these things.

But he was sad that day. So sad that he could not speak. I understood that. I have tried, for years now, to understand everything.

I had thought at the time that he was as he was because of his life. His grey skin and blank conversation. But it was he who said that we are like what we are like, leaving no room for our excuses. But such an emptiness, when it truly belongs to a person, is a strange weight to have to carry beside you. Consequently it felt as though a slow-moving day had hitched a ride on the back of me, or I had hitched on it, for I still cannot tell in which direction I felt his weight most; whether it was before or behind me. A weight, I said, that made me feel like fluid being suctioned through a dark pipe. And he said, life is like that, and that, all love is roadkill. We were, he said, like a too fast car, whose speed came to remove large portions of his being. His stomach, say, or his heart. A hit and run on a quiet street.

You said then that there was nothing to say, nothing to say, and I agreed. You didn't have your glasses on, you said they had disappeared, and you were squinting against the sun. You said you had lost them, you were sure, only because they had been so expensive. I laughed. I knew what you meant, these gross treasures that dematerialise.

We paused a while. Eventually you said you were finding this all very hard to begin. And although I wanted to be there, with you, I was from the very beginning, from the start, already anticipating the end. What it would be like, how it would happen, what would bring us to the point at which we would part.

It had grown cold by then. The sun was on the other side of the harbour. I put my jacket on and pushed my hair out of my face. A young boy came up to us and asked us for money, in return for which he said he'd show us a trick with your matches. I gave him the ten cents in my pocket and he took up the box that you had on the table, holding it between his thumb and forefinger with the match propped against it. He flicked the box into the air and struck the match at the same time, intending to hold the burning match and catch the box in the one hand, but the box opened on the way up and the matches went everywhere. He was embarrassed and bent down and picked up every one even though you told him it did not matter. He left then. We returned to each other. We had both forgotten what it was that we had been saying.

I watched you some years later, going about the day and doing the things you did to fill it, caring for me at the time, and was struck by something in you that was the same as whatever was with you that day, those days, by the harbour, as though something you had forgotten, and forgotten that you had forgotten, had suddenly returned. It was the strange, silent quality of your thought, a sense that there were so many things you did not know how to say. And to be specific, there were not many days down there by the water – two, three, maybe four or five at the most – when we walked there. And although it is clear that each grief is a different thing, the one I recognised in you at the beginning, the one we had at the end, the possibility of encountering and re-encountering it does not seem to leave. Even if we do – leave, that is. As we have. Memory and pain are so strange. And I have seen now how illness, in all its forms, can so completely change a person and spirit them away.

We returned to your room after walking. We slept. We had agreed that we must sleep. I dreamed then that there were no edges to our lips. That when we kissed your mouth moved through my whole body and mine through yours. We began with our lips but the kiss became as big as, if not bigger than, our bodies. It had nothing to do with our mouths and instead it turned our insides out and outsides in, as though we were all wound, like sea anemones at the beach. And in my dream it was night and the whole of the kiss was dark and there was no ground there, there were no borders to our bodies, as though we were all gravity, as well as light.

My mother's face, you said I had. You said I had my mother's face, after all, as though I had tried once to convince you, although I have no recollection of this.

She has a round face, my mother, with what I have always thought of as a heart-shaped chin. It is, indeed, quite beautiful, while my father's face was narrow. It was drawn and weary although still handsome; better-looking, you thought, than how he must have been when he was young. I recall you saying that you hoped you would look rugged and worn like that one day, that you would think your age then a success, even though you had not known him.

You knew my mother though. You saw her with me nearly every week for at least a year. She would come and keep me company, care for me some days when you were at work. She would make me breakfast and lunch and dinner, always so much more than I could eat. My mother. My dear mother.

She was there because she loved me, yes. But she was there because she too was on the run. I didn't mind this, I don't mind this now. In no way do I hold it against her. I know now what it is like to stay somewhere and know you can't possibly remain – there, maybe anywhere – even if you want to.

She had greatness about her and it drove her on. And it drives her still. This huge restlessness of hers that eventually seems to outdo everyone. She didn't leave a trail of people behind her though. Really there were only two. There were others of course but they do not matter. The important ones were my father, and the one after. Then she came to me.

It was storming when she arrived. She had caught a train from the city and then a taxi. I didn't recognise her at first, dressed in a lilac suit with her face hidden behind an umbrella, when she stepped from the car straight into a puddle. Shielding herself, she walked through the wind towards the house. I watched her, half hiding, half waiting to welcome her as she approached, appearing softer at the edges through the paned glass of the door that I stood behind.

My mother was unprepared for such weather, having come from summer in Venice, and in high heels she slipped and tottered in the mud. I let her in and she bundled me up to her. I could smell her sharp perfume and her body bigger than mine. You are terribly thin, she said, but you always were a skinny child. I remember this, the way my buttocks would dig sharply into her lap and she would ask me to get off, my thinness slippery, difficult to hold, like a bundle of twigs that was always catching and escaping.

Come in, come in, I said, and although not offering to take her bag, showed her to the room where she would be sleeping. Don't bother yourself, she said, I won't stay long, I have organised a place in the city. She took her jacket off and hung it over a chair, it was only cotton, and she had been soaked in the short trip to the front door. I suggested she change while I made her tea.

My mother arrived from Venice to take care of me. I had sent her a letter via relatives in Europe, telling her we had moved and that I seemed to be sick. I didn't expect her to come and care for me; she had been gone years. And although I loved her I had become accustomed to not sharing her company. But she came. The man for whom she had spent the last ten years professing the greatest of love was not with her. I asked her where this man had gone, but she was not eager to talk. It was clear that they were no longer together and that he had not returned with her. None of that matters now, she said. She had come only to care for me.

She had brought a present with her. It was folded in the white paper bag that she had bought it in. She never was any good at wrapping, always in such a rush, and when I was a child she'd wrap my birthday presents in alfoil because she would have forgotten to buy paper. It was exciting though – the silver and the sound of it was always exciting. So I had no choice but to tear at it, there was no point in being careful, the way I had to be careful when my presents came in paper – peeling off the tape and folding the wrapping so that it might be used a second time.

This time there was no foil or coloured paper. It was just a white paper bag closed up with sticky tape. Yet it was small, no larger than my hand.

Open it, she said, go on. But I like to wait. This was impossible though, with her standing there at the table while I sat. Open it, she said again, go on. She had brought it, she reminded me, all the way from Venice. And I was afraid of it – afraid that I might not like it, afraid because I wanted it to be right, because it had, as she said, come from so far away.

I lifted off the sticky tape. I put my hand into the paper bag. I took out a fold of tissue paper and opened it.

She had brought me a string of blue glass beads. The light caught on them, they were beautiful. They were threaded with blue string and gold and inside they looked like water where the glass had melted and hardened around air.

Try them on, she said, try them on. I undid the clasp and lifted them to my neck.

Here, let me, and my mother came up behind me, her fingers brushing against my skin as she moved my hair out of the way. I heard the clasp click closed and felt the glass beads against my skin. They were cool, and heavier than I expected.

Let's have a look, she said, and walked around to stand in front of me. They look beautiful, she said, they do look beautiful.

They were lovely. But I wondered why she would buy me blue when she knew I preferred red.

I touched my hand to them, smooth and bright, and when I swallowed I could feel them press against my throat while my mother fluttered about me, holding out mirrors and touching me. My hair. My neck.

I was twenty five-years old then. Young enough to still inhabit the world in a certain way, with a certain lightness; old enough to know how to betray this same absence of gravity, and all I could think of in the beginning was his face, mouth, his body, and all the risks, impossible to turn away from, that any two people together entail. We slept little. And in the morning, after staying at his place in the city, I followed him around the house while he prepared for work, imagining then, despite everything, how easy it might have been to leave. I was looking for something perfect. I know. Aside from any other mess our worlds might have been in, it seemed as though it was that desire which would be my, our, undoing.

I wanted to be everything, and I wanted him to be the same. I knew, know, this to be a ridiculous wish. I warned him once, one of those days when we tried to warn each other of all our faults – tell me your vices, he said – that I was ambitious and that I wanted an excessive amount from my life, and from the lives I shared. I could imagine then, already, waking one morning and saying to him that I was sorry, terribly sorry, but he was no longer what I wanted. I do not know what I want. I imagined that I might one day leave and keep going and going, hunting something that I knew could only elude me.

And one day I might wake again and find I had ceased to hope like I did then, like I still do.

We never know, do we, what it is that we've got. And while we are losing something we don't know what that means either. And then it is gone. And then we know. Maybe you are right, maybe it does all come down to absence. That we live from absence, write from absence, love from it, this empty thing that is always there.

At the jetty where we waited for the ferry in the morning we looked out across the harbour. You had taken the day off work and we were going to the beach. You had called in sick. You did not want to do this. I asked you to. I even said that I would lie for you. No, you said, that would be worse.

We sat on a seat in the sun and, squinting against the sky, could make out a group of people standing at the top of the Harbour Bridge. They were thin dark things from such a distance and we couldn't see how it was that they got up there. They must have climbed, there must be a ladder. You can take tours, you said, and you can see right across the city and to the mountains. You could never do that, you said, you would be terrified. I said I thought I could. We watched them. We did not speak. We could see them being buffeted by the wind and after some time they began to descend, walking slowly down the other side of the arch.

The ferry came and we got on. It was just a small boat that would take us across the harbour, under the shadow of the bridge and towards the Quay. We sat at the front of the boat, outside, and leaned over the edge to watch the water. We sat sideways on the wooden seat. I sat in front of you. You were behind.

On the ferry to Manly you explained to me the names of the boats – famous people, swimmers – while I watched the cool green water just under the pier where the sun entered it. I wanted to ask you if you remembered jumping off jetties into water like that, sun-warmed, light and briny, and opening your eyes in it, down there where there was no sound. Sometimes there would be the faint creaking of wood, a boat, the muffled splash of someone else jumping in, but mostly just breath, thick water, thought. The water lapped at the pier and the boat beside us sounded its horn and began moving.

We sat close to each other on the ferry but did not speak. At one point I left you. I let go of your hand and walked up to the railing of the boat. We were sitting at the side and I went up to the front where the wind blew the sea back against me. The stern was crowded with people, taking photographs, holding each other. One woman had a pair of binoculars. I edged myself into a corner and leaned out, looking down at the water and back towards the city. I hoped you would follow me but you didn't. Instead you folded my jumper into a pillow, lay down on the bench and went to sleep.

He told me that day that the water of the harbour takes three years to drain. Three whole years before the old water replaces itself with new. It was a long time, he thought, it was a slow movement of the sea. I had not thought of it, I had not thought of the harbour like the sea as something changing.

We ate lunch sitting on the wall overlooking the beach. The same wall that I had sat on as a child with my mother, eating fish and chips and feeding seagulls. We felt water on us. It came from nowhere. He turned, looked up, there was one cloud above us and it was raining. Not all the clouds, just the one. We did not believe it at first, but it was rain, it was definitely rain – we could see it marking the dry ground, and there was another couple caught under the same cloud. They had come out on the same boat, one of the couples standing at the front holding onto each other. They still looked happy, eating their fish and chips from a paper box. They were married. We knew that; we looked for the rings.

It was odd at first, the rain was somehow annoying – the rest of the beach was in brilliant sun – but then we began to laugh. We laughed and laughed and laughed. It seemed quite ridiculous and quite right that there would be one cloud and it would rain on us.

We walked away from the cloud and along the beach, rolling up our pants so they would not get wet by the sea, but of course they did and you were annoyed at this. I laughed at you, at your crankiness, at your saying that it was a stupid thing to roll one's pants at all because even if one does they always get wet anyway.

It was dark by the time we went to catch the ferry home. There were hundreds of us, all crammed in together waiting for the boat. There were people in front of us kissing, beside me a woman in yellow sandals, and I could feel someone's arm touching mine. The gangway opened up with the clanking of metal hinges and bars and two men in blue ran out to secure the incoming ferry to the wharf. As we began shuffling towards the gangplank, a murmur moved through the crowd. On the top ramp the people at the front of the line were running – a man with a small child, a woman in an orange sari.

The couple that had been caught under the cloud with us were returning on the same boat. I watched them find their seats inside while we decided to sit out.

In the night sky the first star appeared and I pointed to it, and you said how it was strange, strange to think that what we were seeing no longer exists. I know how a star sucks time around it until it neither gives nor receives light. So space inverts itself. I had read about this. This is how it is. There can be no healing. The body's own black ingestion that says to someone, eventually, yes, I'll let you put your heart there, and then swallows it.

It was in an outdoor café at Manly where he said to me I know, I know what I do – that I give myself to you, only to take myself away.

And I came to do the same. I offered myself; I took myself away. In sickness and in health. I know what I do. I know what I'm doing to you, he said.

The dreams had begun by then. Although we did not recognise them at first. Strange, how sometimes one can be so far into a thing before it is even known the thing is there, for I only realised what they were when he asked me if I was having nightmares because, he said, I had been talking and moving about in my sleep. I said I wasn't; I didn't call them nightmares because they didn't scare me, not in the way one is frightened by bad dreams as a child, shaken and haunted, but I could not bring myself to tell him what it was that I saw, to say that I had shot a woman he once loved and that she didn't bleed, instead she floated in dark space like a hologram, like a double-exposed picture, both red and green, the edges of her body blurred and multiplied and she did not scream. For it was I who was shocked by the shooting, not her, as though she did not mind dying, as though she had been dead all along. It felt instead as though I was the one who had been suddenly and violently killed. I felt myself retreat, and the scene retract, as it was taken over by another – limbs, legs and arms, stumps of things torn off, and again, like his old lover, they floated in dark space, coming closer to me and then away like driftwood, like old rubbish, bottles, floating in the sea.

There was, again, very little blood, they were dead, quite dead limbs. This was not what most disturbed me though. No, more than that it was the fact that this was not my dream. He had had this dream before me and had told me – that this was a recurring nightmare of his childhood. And for some reason, somehow, it had come to me. My sleep, mapped out by guttered roads that I moved down, the edges deep and slippery. While outside – when a dog barked, or water ran, I would rise up, as though a corner had been reached, but there was no choice as to which way I would turn or any chance of coming back, rustled by these night noises and colliding in blind alleys with visions of approaching whales, split-bellied and sticky-taped, and a lady who painted wild flowers to her face, cut from the newspaper, yellowed now, and I would swing down away from the corner and back into guttered sleep. As if I were stormwater moving fast in heavy rain and missing the corners, propelled out. Sleep spilling across the road like an accident, like a flood or afterbirth. And I would be then a child again – taking my bike and riding it faster faster and faster down the slope while my father stood at the side, at the side, and waved madly, desperately, trying to get me to stop while I thought he was yelling at me proudly, telling me to go faster and even faster still because it looked like he was smiling but he was not he was screaming, screaming at me to stop because he saw, as one sees in dreams, the end of me, at the end of the road, in the gutter, me and my brand new bike and our snaky tubular bodies all crumpled together.

I would wake then, sit up and press my head against the cold wall, I would walk about, and try to shake the dreams from my body and he would come to me with a flannel for my face and a towel. A clean shirt. A glass of water on a saucer. Water on a saucer. I had never known this before.

After he left for work I would sit by the window in our bedroom. Each day I was left alone. I had always liked being alone, it was what I had always done, but he was concerned for me – concerned that I might be lonely or frightened. I would reassure him that I was quite fine, really I was, and he would say that he thought of me all day. He said that he worried, and would often phone at noon to speak to me, talking briefly about the proceedings of his day, his lunch and what time he thought he might be home.

In the bedroom there were two windows. The bed was beside one and an armchair beside the other. It was my favourite armchair – a deep red seat and a high back, the grey and blue stuffing coming through the fabric that presented a pattern of embossed red flowers held together by diamonds. It used to be in the living room until he declared it had become unsightly and that he would much prefer it thrown out. It was only taking up space, he said, and did not match the rest of the furniture.

There was this one time in our lives when he developed a sudden passion for matching things; that we should have two armchairs instead of one, and that they should match the lounge, insisting on this theory despite the fact that we did not have the means to realise it. So I had him move the armchair to the bedroom beside the window, and this is where I sat, tracing the flowers, tracing the diamonds, tracing the flowers again.

A woman had moved in next door. From my armchair I could see her in the garden, hanging out washing. She carried it in an old cane basket fraying at the handles and the wind was pushing her blonde hair into her face. I had not met her before and called out. She didn't hear at first and I called again. She heard me the second time and was surprised, she said she didn't realise anyone was home. We spoke a little, me from the window, her outside, and she invited me over for tea. Her name was Isabel.

Already I thought she was beautiful. She wore summer clothes despite it being cold – a blue dress with small white spots on it, black boots – and she wore rings on her fingers. Inside, I watched her moving about the kitchen with ease, although she said it had been years since she had been back there. It was one of those things, she said, where she left the place and returned, left again and returned, to live alone in a house, which, she said, was far too big for one. There was a telephone, but no television, a piano against the living room wall and above it a framed black and white photograph of two children holding each other. Yours? I asked. She laughed. No, my sister and me, she said.

The kitchen in her house was cold. The floor was covered in linoleum and the walls were fibro. It was an old house, she said, and impossible to keep warm. We sat at the table with an electric heater on the floor. There was a white bowl of pears on the table. I'd ask you to stay for a meal, she said, twisting a piece of fruit by its stalk, except that I have to go out.

Where to? I asked.

Work, a restaurant. I serve drinks and dance there.

Like cabaret?

No, she said, pushing her chair back and getting up to fill the kettle again. The room was dark although it was light outside, and as she stood before the sink reaching to twist the tap off, the window sun played at the edge of her arm.

You don't work? she asked, turning to me. I told her that I was not well.

Oh, she said, I'm sorry to hear that. She would not have guessed it, though, by the way I looked.

How do I look? I asked.

She paused then, stepped back towards the bench and considered me. I remember the orange curtains against the window, and how they had faded. I was looking past her, towards these curtains as she replied.

Lovely, she said, you look lovely.

I stayed looking at the curtains and then lowered my eyes because I didn't know why she said this, I didn't know why she lied.

They did not know what was wrong with me. Every test came back negative.

What is it that you want to find? he asked me at the time.

Anything, I answered. If it could be anything at all.

I went to the doctors again and again; they sat at their desks with their yellow paper and illegible writing, looking down before throwing me a question. Pain? And where? With me, pointing – and them, granting one glance before returning to their paper. Pens down, they would turn towards me and with their hands in their lap they look. Yes. This is me. They could draw no conclusions. They would stand then, come up behind me and I would feel hands come to my neck and my jaw, like a loved one about to fix my hair, then I would feel them move to my glands, my throat.

I was tired by doctors, they made me tired, and they would test my blood and test it and test it again. It was a different doctor I went to the next time. She was young and nervous and from the start I did not trust her. She looked at my referral and said that there were a great deal of tests to do, that she would need to take a lot of blood. I nodded, I was used to this. I rolled up my sleeve and she tied and tightened the belt around my arm. I squeezed my fist as she looked for a vein. She could not find one. She pulled the belt tighter around my bicep, as tight as it would go, and told me to clench my fist again. I was clenching my fist. I clenched it and clenched it and could feel the blood suck away and make my arm weak. The doctor pressed at the inside of my arm, my elbow, still trying to find a vein. She thought she had it then and holding one finger in place she fixed the needle. I looked away, already expecting the sight of blood, for I could see the doctor bent up in concentration, still trying to get the needle right. It jabbed in then and hurt, sharper than other times, and it did not feel right, I could feel the point digging at my skin, it hadn't found a vein, I could feel that it had not found a vein, there was no blood, there was not that quiet suck suck that should come, I knew, as blood leaves me. She could not get it, she said, the needle was too big and she pulled it out. Holding her finger over the spot, she pressed on it. I will need the other arm, she said, but my head was reeling and my stomach, I could feel my throat tightening.

I went cold then and dark; there were no noises behind my head, no sense of a body, although there were fireworks, and some bright light, blue, behind my eyes, and I was a long way, such a long way it was so far, but without weight, without time. Then came a sound of static, followed by the voice of the doctor, I remembered her, her mouth moving above me and the light bulb too bright, so bright I closed my eyes, and I could feel her hand on me, somewhere, helping me, I could feel her helping me, trying to help me up – no, I am trying to get up but she is holding me saying, stay still, don't move, just lie there a while and someone will come and pick you up, take you home – take me home, someone will come now and take me home, home I think, I think of home.

I have a photograph, taken from inside our house and looking out across the lake. It is dark inside, the picture is a little blurred – as though a child had taken it – the framing of the subject all wrong, neither taking a picture of the inside of the house nor the outside. It is more a blur of dark and a blur of light. There are two windows, side by side, looking out across the grass towards the water and the photograph is divided into four by this frame – the cross-section of the window dividing the photo in half.

This is what draws my attention first – the wooden window frame, the sense of a dark house, and even though it is not what is pictured, the photograph puts me there – behind the window, looking out towards the lake. It evokes for me more clearly than any picture of myself everything that we were before. Especially because there is no one in the photograph, especially because there is just an eye behind the lens.

The water stretches out towards the right and beyond. It is still, it looks cold, like frosted glass, ice, even concrete. There is no sign of movement. No swimmers, no birds or geese. Behind the lake is a strip of sand, trees, bushland, stretching out and around the water. It is out of focus. Only the window frame is sharp. The sky, as I said, is white. It looks glary, wintertime with the sun fighting to get through. And it is scratched, the whole corner that includes the lake looks scratched. I hold the picture closer, I have become shortsighted since then, and I realise it is because the window has a flyscreen attached to it on the outside. This part of the picture, the water and the trees, was taken through a fine mesh. If I look even closer I can make out the dirt on the glass – the windows are not well kept, I can make out spots and dust, the grit lodged at the edges. This is the inside of the house.

You said to me once that you were relieved you had not documented your life in photographs. You had none of yourself, neither had you taken any of those whom you loved. You had never even owned a camera. I could not conceive of this, I could not conceive that you would not want to remember, or at least have them and hide them away – not wanting to remember, but because of that desire, and because of their invisible existence, you would remember all the same. The containment of memory was simply not an issue for you. Your past never seemed to be something you returned to. It was never entirely dead or alive in the way a photograph both kills and recalls things.

Illness becomes like this, like his unremembered memory, retaining no pictures of its sensation and its effects and unable to be anything other than the fluidity that the past is contained within. It is sediment, for although it might appear dead and gone, it retains, always, some form in the potential of its return. It is how the past exists, but it cannot be what the past is.

And as with pictures so you were with music – you were never bothered by a song, you could listen to anything and it never reminded you of your past, it never upset or delighted you like that. It never took you back to things that you used to be.

I am the opposite. For the most part, everything reminds me of something else. Music can upset me for days. As a child my mother told me I was highly strung and my aunt said that I was like her and walked about with my heart on my sleeve. Perhaps this is why I have come back to all this just from meeting you on the street. You are a long white bone that does not leave.

I only ever saw two photographs of his. They were of his children. He kept them on the mantelpiece and would pick them up and look at them when he missed them. They were taken with a polaroid camera that he had borrowed from a friend.

I like these kind of photographs. When I was a child polaroid photographs were so exciting and you would take one just to watch its picture happen. It was an intriguing thing – to see the past captured so recently, waiting impatiently for the few minutes it took for the picture to resolve itself in the darkness and come out. And so those pictures of his children, taken quite some time ago, retained an immediacy, having been taken quickly, and without premeditation, while the children did not know.

From the desk in my hotel room I can see ants crawling along the architraves. He told me many times what this type are called but I have forgotten. They are the kind, he told me, that are very difficult to kill. They were often all through the kitchen, looking for honey. I do not know what they hope to find in my room here as there is little food: a few biscuits and some sugar, no bread. I notice that they have spread out into the living area. They crawl in different directions, one line moving towards some biscuits kept on the small coffee table, another moving away. When they meet they stop and appear to touch heads. This moment interests me. I have always, since I was a child, wondered what it is that they tell each other, how they speak. I would like to ask him what he makes of such a moment. They do not appear to speak with every ant they pass. For some they do not even stop. What would he think of this? I do not know.

When we were walking in the first days around the water, that thick dark water, he pointed to a small spot on the horizon at the end of the path, by the rocks. It was a patch of white that turned out to be a woman getting married. Behind her, in the next bay, was a large navy ship, a huge green thing that loomed behind the small white bubble of a woman. The sea was choppy that day and the water was rocking up and hitting against the stone wall. There was white foam tossing about on the ocean, and from such a distance it seemed to merge with the woman in the dress, so that for a moment she appeared to be falling into the sea. We passed her as we continued to walk, she and her entourage approaching from the opposite direction. He said to me then, joking and quietly, for we were within hearing – promise me, he said, that if you ever get married you won't wear a dress like that. I promised. We laughed.

We kept walking. We reached a point where the path along the water was walled off for reconstruction so we took a detour across the grass. It was getting dark by then and the gardens were closing up. Turning, we headed back along the water, passing the point where we first saw the bride. Lights flickered across the harbour and we headed on, past the swimming pool. It was empty at that time of year, May it was, coming into June. We stopped a while to look at it. It is white, you said. You had always thought the bottom of the pool was blue. There were still beach umbrellas, although faded, propped up in the middle of the tables. And there was rainwater in the bottom of the pool and fallen leaves. You said there was something disturbing about an empty pool. I agreed. I said something about how it felt as though there was still a possibility of drowning – but in all that air, in all that white space. A sort of death by hyperventilation. My chest jumped at the thought, and I told you that it reminded me of childhood nightmares in which there was always a large white building and few people. I never knew the way out, although I was aware that outside there was only unbearably bright sun, that I was in some sort of desert and there was, somewhere, following me, some strange man.

You said you wondered why the pool needed to be emptied at all.

I cannot see the water from my window in the hotel. It looks out instead over grey buildings and rooftops. There are a few small back gardens, inner-city rectangles of weeds and chokos, frangipani in the summertime, and I can see washing hanging over a fence. Although I cannot see the water I know where it is and when I wake up and lie in bed I know in which direction it is from me and I imagine it, not far from where I am. I imagine the boats pulling into the harbour. This is one of my favourite things – boats at port, empty or returning, silent and heavy and such huge things that they are frightening to look at, like beasts when they are not in the sea, when they are pulled up on the ground to be repaired and cleaned and they balance there on wooden beams and pulleys, towering above people and I look at them then and am terrified by how deep the sea must be and how heavy a ship is and by how strange it is that they should ever float. You knew this and would go down with me to the harbour so that we could walk along the edge of the water and watch them, beached, forced from the sea.

And in my room, later, in the room from which I watched years and things gather and leave, shadows opened to me – like those of the trees slowly growing on the wall in the evening, the shadow of a bird flight and then the dark, like cold water, entering, and the smell of things. The smell of the room and what belonged to it. Like love – harbouring me; like the light on the back of him as he entered, weary, in the evening. And my waiting. Like all that harbour water in all its patience, resting and ready for the heavy metal of the ships. Waiting to shelter them, to let them come and leave. We are harbouring. The way I am now a ship and he is now a ship and I do not understand either us or the sea.

I am paid now to walk into high-rise office blocks and speak. That is what people want. They seem to want me to solve them. I have one of those large black diaries and, to my horror, a handbag. People listen to me.

Today, as on most days, I walked into a room full of men and women in suits. I sat down at the table. A woman from the front desk brought me coffee. They had been waiting for me. I was late. I said to them, placing my papers before me and taking out my pen, that I thought it time for us to start. I apologise, I said, for my lateness, but you need not have waited for me to begin.

At the start I had two futures, both of which I could see quite clearly. One was concerned with everything that I was when I was with you, while the other had nothing to do with you at all. In the latter future, you were nothing in my life except a memory, something that in some way enabled that future to happen. And so perhaps, in that instance, you had much more to do with me than I might at first have thought; that very ordinary thing of the present depending on the past and the future depending on the present, and vice versa.

I have met up with this future now, although it is, of course, different – but somehow still the same – like an adult version of a child, an old friend found after they had been forgotten. It is what I always knew, as though it had always been waiting to happen, and now that it has the rest of my future feels completely untold, untellable. I have no sense of what it might be the way I once did.

I am everything I ever was or might be and I am nothing. These pictures of a future do not and will not ever exist, the way I watch them always from above, or from the side. From somewhere in the air I look down at myself, as though I were dead and alive at the same time. And misrecognising everything. That self I see on the street has her back to me and I have a feeling that were she to turn around in spite of the set pattern of my imagining, she would not be who I thought she was at all. As though I were my own dead friend who, for a brief second, I think I see again. I find it very strange when this happens, when I am sure that I am seeing someone whom I know is dead and for the whole time, although the time is always so brief, I know absolutely that I am seeing them and that I am absolutely not. It is the greatest moment of both faith and dis-belief, and it felt something like this when I saw you on the street.

It was not working any more. We both knew that, even if I loved you. It was never something anticipated – reaching a point where the sentiment of love was not enough. I always thought it would be but it was not. It was simply that I needed to lead my life differently, and at the same time, although you did not say it, your life would, I imagine, have been better without me. That sickness, so often un-named between us, had been a long thing, and although it felt as though it was lifting a little, we were both tired by its length and its weight.

It is such a peculiar thing, to leave something that is loved, to love it and leave it anyway, living with it and without it for a long time, for such a long time. For we let each other go. Let go now, go. I would have followed you on the street that day if I could. I have always wanted to – follow someone, that is – someone whom I imagine to be far more than what they are. To be secretive and obsessed like that. But I didn't. I couldn't. Besides, it was busy and there were too many people and it was only a matter of seconds before I lost sight of you in the crowd.

Once you had disappeared I turned and walked back the way I had come. I stopped at the steps of the

Town Hall and sat down. It was sunny there, it was always sunny there and there were always people – waiting, doing nothing, talking. I had passed often on the bus or on foot and wondered what it was that people did there, how they came to be there, the way I found myself there then, sifting through the immediate and distant past as though my whole present had become a disembodied moment that I had in fact foreseen – as if all the time before it and all the future was my real life that might make some sense of the one moment that had just passed. But it was not the case; not then anyway. For it is, I know, impossible to force a life into resolution; unlike the way time is forced to resolve itself; obeying the form and transience of its own body. One minute belongs to one minute, an hour to an hour. But we are not like this, we don't know what it is that we belong to, and time cheats us, it refuses us – refuses admittance after hours, refuses our desire to delay – and is a force with which we share nothing but emptiness and passing.

Was it a fateful day? Perhaps. A mistake? Most certainly; that meeting we had, so briefly, on the sidewalk of George Street. But does an act of fate and the moment of accident exclude one another? I don't think so. There, the sun came and went again. Clouds moved overhead with the breeze and as they passed they took the light, just like that, took the shadows too and then gave them back again.

I was in my black woollen jacket and I buttoned it up as we were speaking although it was not that cold. You squinted when the light came and it looked as though you were smiling but I was not sure. It was not a recurring moment of knowing from some time before that we would separate and meet again that consumed me in those small moments, it was not as simple as that. And yet I recognised the scene that occurred. A premonition? I don't know, and I try not to partake in the question of destiny too frequently. Perhaps, I thought, it was the jacket, the way, with a new and treasured item, one imagines oneself wearing it, carrying out the day's activities, or saving it for some special occasion. In such a new and lovely coat I wore it along with everything I thought I could become inside it. And I know I imagined I could speak to you – I had not stopped this, imagining our conversations, although I knew I would, stop imagining you, eventually. So I buttoned up my coat while you spoke, recognising your habit of repeatedly pushing your sunglasses back up the thin bridge of your nose.

There are spaces, preserved by every person I have taken and been taken into. They open up again. And close. And sometimes, like then, like when we met then so briefly on the street, I knew that I would do this – open what had been open for you before – but only once, and would not ever do it again. In those few minutes you were absolutely present and yet became an absolute memory. Like a photograph and a reflection, inescapably different and the same. For you were, up until then, an apparition pertaining to my future, someone I knew I would one day again meet, and yet by meeting I found you transfigured into the strange shape that I consider to be the fleet of my history. The street was busy. We were standing in the middle of the footpath. People pushed past us and we did not move aside. I saw you look to the edge where the shops were, where there was some space, but we did not take it.

If I had not grown up being accustomed to looking at photographs as the containers of the past I wonder if my memory would still work like this – in snapshots, in frozen moments, pictures without words. For it was in this moment that the silent memory of my future, of a once possible and since forgotten future, caught up with me. Déjà vu, some would call such an instant – a moment that has been seen before, a moment that is always both a pleasant and unsettling thing – this experience, so fleeting, of knowing you know something so well while at the same time being so unable to place its familiarity, forcing it to exist only as an inexplicable plunge into deep space, with no pattern or recourse to the present, being both so close – so interior – and so strange.

But it was not you that made up that moment. You were already so close and so unfamiliar and I knew this, and I knew how this was so. No, it was something else, an eclipse of the present by our own past, an eclipse that stunned and darkened me but which I could not locate. I had seen this before. I had known. I had always known, that this was coming. The filmic moment when all final and inevitable meetings occur.

But it is their uselessness that plagues me. The uselessness of these seemingly final but indefinitely suspended things. The uselessness of illness, the uselessness of beauty, and our inability to do anything with either of them other than to witness them and take them as we can. I cannot do anything with our past other than remember it. As though it were some quiet and shining temple that I can turn to only via something that resembles my own heart. We are not each other's lives now, illness is not my life now, yet inevitably these things always are, as though they are simply rooms in my own house that I will keep returning to.

This was the anticipated future that I was brought back to. It was the image of a future that I had created in my past, right down to my black coat. I had always wanted a black coat like the one I was wearing then, and, as is the way with such things, I liked it far more when I did not have it than when I did. For once I had it, it did not solve any of the problems that I encountered whilst wearing it and yet it had held the hopes of so many things, of letting me become so many things. Such is the magic of production, the mystery we give to what we come to possess. But it had no pockets. That was its one fault. I could not hide my hands.

I exist, we exist, only in the past, however much it is present, however much memory might be a live wire. You are a dead ear now into which I speak and between the two – my voice and you – there is this time delay, this wrenching of space that prevents, always, the meeting of our speech.

You said that you needed to find another job if we were going to be able to keep paying the rent on top of my various treatments, doctors and medications. You didn't want to, you said, but thought at the same time that you must, that it would be good for you – we both knew – if you had more to do, if you did not think you had to stop your life for me. Besides, you said, there are enough people here wanting to look after you. You meant my mother; later you would mean Isabel too, but really you meant my mother. You didn't think she should be there as often as she was, and when she was not there you would do everything, run my bath, wash me, brush my hair and dry it so that I would not catch cold. You would make me food and bring it to me in bed and when

I was feeling well you would take me outside and we'd walk a little. I taught you how to plait my hair. You liked doing this, you would ask me sometimes if you could, brushing it carefully and parting it down the middle with your finger. You'd divide it into two and make a plait on either side, or sometimes you would just do one at the back. You would do this very slowly and very carefully and you would call them braids.

To apply for the job he bought a new suit, his interview suit. It was black and the jacket did up to his chest and there were four buttons at each wrist. My mother had ironed his shirts and he hated this. But he looked handsome all the same and I told him so. Dishy, I said, you look dishy. Dishy? Yes, and we laughed. My mother told him that he should comb his hair too, his dark hair that he preferred untidy, brushing it through with his fingers. Do you even own a comb? she asked. No. She found it difficult to tolerate this and I could hear her afterwards, muttering. Inevitably she bought one for him and brought it with her the next time she came, although he refused to use it.

He looked worried when he left that day and I wished him luck although I knew he didn't believe in it nor did he really want the job. It was not that particular job he didn't want, nor even his current one. It was more that he would have preferred not to have had to have a job at all. The one he was applying for was an administrative position, where he would deal all day with phone calls and paper, but it paid more than the one he had. He thanked me for the luck anyway and ran down the stairs; just the glint of his white cuffs and collar and then he was gone. Strange, how some images last – the way his body, as it descended the stairs, was taken up by shadow and the green light of morning like water, and it was just those white bands of brightness and the side of his face that I saw leaving, going out into a world with which I no longer conversed.

I thought often, when I was ill, of that water – the harbour near his city house, which we used to walk around. I thought of its cold blackness and the steady lapping and glittering beneath the city lights. The way its body was always gently moving and bubbling, always ebbing. Like our bodies when they were together, the way they were when we tried to sleep. The way that water seems forever to be both finding and losing itself, never the same. There is always a loneliness about the sea, even that tame water in the harbour, and I would think of it – way out, beyond the sight of land, where the ocean is always moving and always too deep.

It was often late when we walked down that way. I recall one particular night when there was no moon, the sky pale instead with city lights, and there was a cold wind. I could hear the boats rocking and clicking in the water. Further out there was dance music coming from a ship.

The tide is high, he said. We stood against the railings and leaned into the breeze and he told me how, when he was younger, he used to steal boats at night and row them way out into the deep.

We walked along the water's edge then, following the fence until it ran out and met rock. I walked farther, closer to the end, and looked down into the sea. It was black and rocked up against blacker stone, shiny and cold in the night and I edged myself farther and farther towards it without realising. Behind me he leaned against the corner of the fence and looked out. The wind was blowing in his face and he was farther from me than I could easily reach. I stepped back from the edge and moved towards him. We held our heads together, the bones of our foreheads touching, like the black rocks blackened and washed by the water, hard and close in the night, not quite swallowed by the sea. I could feel the night coming into my ears and wrapping my scarf about my head we squatted on the ground. There, he said, pointing to a small white yacht rocking in the water, there are people in there. We watched it, and every now and then there would be some light coming from its window and we would glimpse bodies moving inside before it fell dark again. We watched them until it grew too cold and the night grew lighter and orange in the city. We held each other's arm then and walked up the hill towards home.

Things are different now. Before it all, we embarked on what felt at the time to be what would become the rest of our lives. We began, we knew, something that would one day complete itself – finishing eventually, but it seemed, or it was hoped, that when that finally happened, we, each of us, would be completed and finished with it.

It is different now. His life is separate from mine and moving. Or part of it is, it seems. I did not know for how long the sickness would go on and I anticipated a time when, if it did not ease, I would need to tell him that he was free to leave, the way we had agreed at the beginning – that each of us would always be free to leave.

It was not like that then, I knew, but I had to think about these things. My future, it felt, had been pushed into a period of postponement. My life, although it had started, was again waiting to begin.

He came home in the evening and said that he did not think he had got the job. He told me this when we were alone, preparing for bed. He had been quiet all through dinner and I guessed this was what was wrong but I didn't ask. My mother was there and it could have been her cooking, he was always afraid of her cooking – that it would be too good and he would eat so much that he would appear gluttonous, or it would be too salty and he would not eat enough. He knew there could be no right way with her.

Don't tell your mother, he said to me, about the interview, she already thinks that there is quite enough that I cannot do. True, he didn't really want the job in the first place, but it is always a good feeling to succeed at something whether your heart is in it or not, and he would have liked this sense of success and would have enjoyed, also, joking over the fact that the success was empty and that he had succeeded anyway.

That isn't true, I said, about my mother not approving of him, but we knew it was a lie. She is my mother, I said, after a while, that is all; that was the only thing I could say. For my mother was coming regularly each week to see me. And it was not that he disliked her; he was fond of her, he admired her, bold, he called her. Saying it from a distance, for the boldness of a partner's mother is something, he felt, that could be admired but which he had no desire to embrace.

She had caught the train up from the city that day, as she usually did when she visited me, and had walked to our house from the station, arriving in her coat, the woollen one, chequered and wet-smelling with large green buttons that were always done up. Even if it was not raining her coat smelled wet. I know this because whenever she came she would hug me and hold me to her with my face pressing against her wetsmelling breast and the green buttons.

She took off her coat when she arrived and unpacked her bag. She always had a bag with her, filled with food and books, with things she thought I might need. Today she had brought me music. I loved it when she brought me music. She brought Schubert,

Schumann, Bach and played them just a little at a time on a cassette player. She would sit down to them and listen. I liked this, I liked this very much. I liked it even more when she cooked while she played music, humming a little, moving about. It surprised me though, to see her cooking. I told her this; I didn't think she did that sort of thing, I said. Well, she said, things change. But it was not that. She is warm in her own way, but not domestically like that. You are my daughter, she said, that is why I am doing this, touching her face as she passed the hallstand mirror, a handsome face still, her clean eyes. It was one of symmetry, and she had once said that she thought she'd have made a good man – not that she wanted to be a man for she was a woman and there was, undoubtedly and unavoidably, a womanliness about her – one that did not wish to grow old and fade as the aged do, no, touching her face there, just lightly beneath the cheekbone, eye wrinkles, no.

Where, though, was the man she loved? I asked. It made no sense that she had returned alone. She made as if not to hear, returning to the kitchen to pull out pots and pans, complaining about the state of our cupboards. I told her that I saved them just for her, knowing that cleaning them would occupy her for at least a day. I waited for a response but there was none. I retreated to my room.

I have one photograph of them together, my mother and her love, before they were together. It was taken at Caves House, when we lived there and it was my mother's job to tend to the rooms and the breakfast tables.

On the back of the photo is scribbled in ink: *Five Tourists and Dog, Posing.* My mother, though, is not part of the tour group and I am not sure how she came to be in it. No one is smiling. Even the dog looks glum. The ladies in their white dresses are perched on cold damp rocks and they do not look eager to remain. To the right of the photograph sits a well-dressed man in a dark suit and hat, leaning one hand on an umbrella as the tip digs into the ground.

This was my mother's love.

A small dog, a Jack Russell, sits beneath his knee. It is slightly blurred, the dog, having moved just as the shutter closed. My mother sits beside the well-dressed man. Her hand rests on his shoulder. She looks stunned, which is unlike her, for she is so fond of being photographed. It was my father who took the picture, purposely early I think, before anyone was quite ready, so that no one, particularly my mother, could, on reflection, consider themselves too beautiful. In fact they all look decidedly uncomfortable, including the dog. It would not have been unlike my father to have made some smart remark a moment before the shutter closed in order to bring on the slightest of confusion and hence cause frowns. He saw the gesture of his wife, he saw her hand resting on the other man's shoulder.

She should have left my father long before she did. Not because he had done anything wrong, but because it was quite clear that she did not, or did no longer, love him. He adored her though, and at the time, and for quite some time, that was what she wanted.

But in the evenings sometimes she would take the visitors' book to her room and, sitting at the dressing table that doubled as a writing desk she'd read through the week's entries, scanning the names, checking for anyone famous. And whenever the opportunity arose she would remind us that even the queen had been. My mother. Who, had she not married a man in love with such a far away place, might have been the famous singer she always dreamed of being.

When she finally left, with me bundled in the car beside her, and drove to the shack she had bought by the river on the coast, her own mother said it was an act of madness, that the altitude of those mountains had finally gone to her head. Too much air, my grandmother said, sitting with her lap full of wool. She told us that it could weaken the system, that it thinned you out. It was essentially a fault of character, she said, although not one inherited, that caused my mother to leave.

The man she fell in love with was not originally part of her plan. She was not following anyone when she moved into that river house. He arrived, months later, only by a series of coincidences. He said he had been driving down that way anyhow and thought he'd stop by for a drink. It was evening when he arrived and he accidentally left the car lights on. When he went to leave he found the battery dead. My mother didn't have a car at the time, so he could only wait for the bus that came three times a week to take him the sixty kilometres to the city. He arrived on a Monday evening and the bus was not due until Wednesday.

He phoned his wife, explained, said he was staying in a hotel. When he got off the phone he assured my mother that he no longer loved that woman. But I remember that he still called her his wife while he bargained over another one.

I sat on the floor, colouring a picture, softly, so that I could hear what they said. My mother stayed silent, staring at the table, then looked up. She asked if he was hungry. She went to the fridge and stared into it, still waiting for his response. It was summer and she was wearing a thin dress that I could see him staring through. There was sunburn on her cheeks. Yes, he said, watching the back of her, he was a little. He moved up behind her and while she continued to stare vacantly at the cold food he kissed her on the back of the neck. She turned to him and, leaning her head against the freezer door, told him that he could have fried eggs or cheese on toast. We've already eaten, she said, closing the fridge behind her as he moved back and pushed his hands into his pockets.

My mother did tell me his name once but I have forgotten it. It is irrelevant anyway, for I never called him by anything, and the two of them referred to one another only by pet names, such as honey and love. Although there must have been a real name – even if I did not know it – the name of the man she fell out of love with, the name of the man who stayed, with whom she stayed, for lack of anything better, for fear, for the hope that it might come to something else.

He stayed that Wednesday, Friday, the following Monday, even though each of those days the bus could have taken him back to the city. The grocery boy delivered the food on Thursday, and my mother, having expected him to be gone, hadn't changed the order. So I had cereal for dinner while he ate the eggs, all the eggs.

My mother liked to think he was the reincarnation of the great musician, Satie. She said she was only joking, and perhaps she was, but we each knew how easy and serious it was to accidentally harbour an affection for one person because they reminded you of another. It was quite clear though to anyone who chose to look that this man was not Satie. We had first seen him playing piano in the dining room of Caves House in the evenings. My mother would take me often to listen to him, playing Satie's music adequately on an old, slightly out of tune piano, and although he obviously loved the music (there look, oh, my mother would say, he's closing his eyes) he was not brilliant. He was an ordinary man with an ordinary passion. But my mother did not understand this.

She loved the real Satie. The story of his compositions more than anything, wandering through the night, writing a bar beneath each streetlight and wandering again. But such a difficult man to live with, she'd say, as though she knew.

This was what she said about all brilliant men, with a slight spite fused with regret due to the thought that her present life was not difficult because of one. She could excuse difficulty if it was due to brilliance, but boredom was different. She would sigh then, not seeing in herself the equivalent as a difficult woman.

And so my mother came to look after me. I could hear her footsteps nearing my room before she entered it; where she took the ironing board from the closet and pulled out the shirts that were kept crushed in the bottom drawers.

When is he due home? she asked me. Him. Ironing a straight crease down the length of a sleeve.

I don't know.

She wants to know though – how we manage this. How we have managed up to this point, prior to her arrival. We make do, I said, as she buttoned up the cuffs and the collar and placed the shirt on a metal hanger, carefully, in the wardrobe. Shirt after shirt after shirt, like mirror apparitions in their dark box.

She understood my answer. The self-sufficiency of care. Yes, of course, she said.

In the morning when he left for work, to his old job that he did not want, I walked him to the door where he kissed me. I am not as tall as he is and when he moved his head back from me my eyes were level with his neck and I could see a small spot of blood where he had cut himself shaving. He kissed me again and left and I listened to his footsteps as they moved away.

I lay back in bed then and remembered. Thought of my body like dark water filling the time of day. A desk we shared faced the window in the bedroom. It had become mine. The whole room had become mine; its blue vase, its books and furniture. I watched the desk from the position I had resumed in bed and considered moving towards it. He had said I needed to find something to do all day, that I could not keep sitting and waiting. He gave me paper and pastels and suggested I draw. What though? I asked. Anything, he said, anything at all.

In his absence I would wait for Isabel's arrival. She would come and keep me company when neither he nor my mother were there. I loved it when she came. She would breeze in, always light, her thin cotton shirt fluttering as she moved. I thought about her all the time. I wondered what the rest of her life was like. I wanted to tell him everything she said. I wanted to show him how she danced, and all the dresses she wore, and the pink hat, like that of a cowgirl, that I had seen sitting on top of her cupboard. She had a handbag. I admired this then –

I did not know how one became a woman with a handbag. At the time I was not one. He didn't care. He thought handbags were ridiculous and that women only lost things in them.

Doesn't she have anything else to do with her day? he asked when I told him how we had spent all afternoon by the lake. I don't know, I said, I didn't ask. In fact I had hardly asked her anything. We had struck something. Something new and fresh between us. She made me laugh, and it was as if we were afraid to ask anything more of one another, afraid of some greater closeness, direct and articulated. We were new things. No. I do not know what else she does, I said to him. I knew strangely little about her life.

I turned to look out the window. The wind had swept half the leaves from the trees; on the mulberry bush, the few remaining had turned yellow and the sun shone through them. The trees' thin branches twisted every which way as though they were weeds under water. There was a currawong perched on one. It leaped off and dropped, swiftly, its whole weight plummeting straight down before its wings opened and it took to flight.

Isabel was coming over in the morning, she said she would be there by eleven and maybe we could have lunch. I listened for her coming, her footsteps on the dirt path, her voice calling out. Hello, she called. Are you home? You, she called me, you. I am the only one she came to see. Yes, I called back, I'm here, come in. I was in the kitchen, already waiting for her.

She came in, kissed me lightly on the cheek and turned on the radio. She was happy that morning; some mornings she was so terribly happy and she looked like summer. Come here, she said, reaching her hands towards me. Come here. There was music playing, softly, soft enough so that we could still speak and she began to sway to it, moving about the room. She was laughing as she showed me the way a child moves, like I did, she said, delightfully, she said. Like this, and showed me to myself, turning and turning, spinning like a child, giddy and awkward, and then faster, until she became so dizzy that she nearly fell and slipping a little, grabbed at the corner of the table. Come here, she said, try this, laughing, but I was weak. She took one of my hands in hers and held her other hand to my back and began to move towards me and away, then side to side. I tried to move in the way her body suggested but I was awkward; it was not like before when movement would come to me without thinking. Don't try, don't try to move, she said then. Come closer, follow me.

Is this how you do it in the city? I said.

No, not like this. I could feel her legs against mine, her body, her chest, and she was holding me and swaying and swaying me with her and I no longer had to make any effort to move. She took my body and made it dance for me.

I could feel my stomach breathing against her, I could feel myself leaning against her and she didn't seem to mind. She said to stand on top of her feet. I did, I lifted one foot and placed it, followed by the other, and like this she waltzed me slowly and stiffly around the room with the sides of our heads pressed together like the point of a fulcrum. I could smell her hair. And with my ear against her face like that I could hear her voice muffled through the thickness of her cheek. Her skin was cool, my ear felt cold against it and I gave her all my weight. That's the way, she said, that's the way.

Then she sat me down in my chair and then she left.

And the next thing I knew was the end of the day, staring at me like an obvious thing misplaced.

I dreamed last night of how long my hair would be when I next saw him. It would be long. It would be really long. It would be all the way down to the back of my knees. And thick. As thick as a horse's tail.

It did not used to be like this, although it had always been long. I kept it long until I left him and then I cut it off. Women do this sort of thing. Cut off their beauty because someone loved it once. It was useless by then though. My hair was not lovely like it was in the dream. When I was ill much of it had fallen out and it was very thin by the time I left him. When he ran his fingers through it he would come out with handfuls of hair and you could see the white beginnings of my scalp.

When my mother noticed this happening she brought me a present. My mother loved presents. Again she did not wrap it, she said it was not really a gift. She handed me a brown paper bag. I looked inside. She had put a plait of hair in it. It was not her hair, she said. I could see that. It was the wrong colour – light brown instead of dark. She had bought it as a teenager and used to attach it with a bobby pin to her bun so that it would fall all the way past her waist. She said maybe I should cut my hair off and wear the plait instead. But it is the wrong colour, I said, for both of us, for we had the same dark hair. Just for the time being, just for the time being, she said. As though time were something that could hold still and be, and not something, like being, that had passed and would keep passing.

I put the plait back in the bag and said that I would not wear it.

There is a movie being shot in the street outside my hotel today. There have been signs stuck up on the lampposts for the last week, saying that on Wednesday parking will be prohibited. Today is Wednesday. There are some cars but not where the signs are. And although I have been looking out for famous actors I haven't yet seen any.

This morning an ambulance drove up and parked, drove up and parked, drove up and parked with its siren on. I imagine that this scene will be in the movie, that one instance out of the three will be chosen. The ambulance parked and the driver got out, came around to the back and opened the doors. She pulled out a white stretcher bed but there was no one on it. The sick or injured person must be inside the block of apartments across the street. Part of the movie must be about how they were hurt and how they get help, if they live or die. I wonder if the movie crew will come back tomorrow, if there will be actors then, rehearsing on the street. I hope this will be the case. I would like to see somebody famous. Not that I would ask them for their autograph. I would just watch from the window and say to people later that I had seen that star, that I had seen them in the flesh.

We used to go to the movies. When we came out one night he said, that was lovely. Which part did you like best? I asked. It was so nice, he said, just to sit for a while in the dark.

I sit now at the table by the window and work for much of the day, and by the afternoon I have seen the star. I fell asleep for some time, for longer than I intended, and when I woke I heard their voices. Loud American voices. Of course, I thought, of course they would have American voices, they are, after all, making a movie, thinking for a moment that they were American voices because I was still in America. But I am not in America. I looked out the window. There were two young women seated on the front steps of the apartment block. They had scripts in their laps and a man was talking to them, pointing, directing. Not far from them, on the pavement, a young man walked back and forth. This was the star, I could tell. This was the man the girls on the steps were waiting for. It was obvious because of his clothes – expensive pants, and just a singlet – and because of the way he walked, strutting, a slight swagger, with his hands in his pockets and his head down, waiting for everyone else to get it right. He wore a hat too, a man's hat, woven out of some soft grass with a leather band about the rim. The kind of hat worn by men older than him, and because of this it only made him look young. It was the kind of hat a gentleman might tip in passing, or remove when speaking to a lady. I could not imagine this man doing any of these things.

But I do not recognise him. I would not be able to say who it was that I have seen, watching the street and waiting. Waiting again for the arrival of a man the way I waited all those years before.

The camera crew have arrived now. They have whole trailers filled with equipment and with their arrival a sense of excitement builds on the street, kids stand at the sidelines, cars are redirected. Even the waiters from a nearby restaurant come out to see. The camera men are wearing headsets and belts. They unload equipment, wire things up. One man carries a pot of fake tulips with a lead running out of it. There must be a microphone in it and I imagine that it will be positioned in the corner of a room so they can capture every word that passes between the man in the hat and one of the women sitting outside in the street. But nothing happens. The actors just keep talking to each other and looking at their pieces of paper.

It was afternoon coming into evening. He was still not home, although he had said he would be, and the insect that I had seen in the morning caught between the window and the flyscreen was moving more slowly, although it continued to try to find a way out. I had looked but I could not find one. By morning I imagined it would be dead.

I walked to the mailbox to collect the mail. This was as far as I would go. There were no letters. The last of the sunlight hit the wood at the back of the box and I thought at first that it was a yellow envelope but it was not. I walked back down the drive. There were pockets of air that still smelled of morning. A coming of winter morning, of fires put out but continuing to smoulder in the cold, while across the valley the sun began to sink. On the road boys raced their push-bikes with drink cans wedged between the spokes so they rattled and scraped as they sped down the hill.

When he drove out that morning I watched him from the window. There was a breeze and it tossed the leaves about. He drove over one on his way out. Just one. It was small and brown and fell from the tree as he was driving. I saw it coming, as if it were a bird, I saw it coming and hoped it would move away in time because I knew he wouldn't stop and I didn't want him to crush it but it came down, touched a corner of itself on the ground lifted up again and went down and up and under – onto the street and beneath the wheels of the car. I did not hear a thing though. I tried not to let myself even imagine a sound.

It was dark when the wind came, the weather always a stranger to itself, always a surprise, and it rattled the windows. Then it blew them, blew them so they sounded like drums, the glass thumping the frame and again as another gust came, coming from some long way away and coming closer and closer so that it sounded like an engine and my stomach turned because it sounded like a car, his car, and I thought, finally – he has arrived but he hadn't, he was not there yet and I did not know where he was, and it was just me and the wind and the glass shaking and thudding in its frame. Love, it said, it was Love, hitting its head against the wall.

I was alone and it was night. Isabel had already left for the city. I saw her as she got into her car. She had a white dress on and lipstick. She had gold shoes.

I looked out into the night and thought of him asking me once if, from the window, I could see the trees. He was there too, beside me, with his eyes closed. He wanted to lie there blind, and have me tell him what the darkness of the night looked like.

He had promised though, he had promised that he would not be late.

I pressed myself closer to the window. There were insects on the other side. I listened for his car, his footsteps, waiting for him to come home, eat a little, and, once I had gone to bed, to sit in the living room and read.

It had been dark for a long time when he finally arrived. He looked tired. He said it had been a long day. His skin looked thick with the grit of the city and when she came closer she could smell it on him.

Where have you been?

Nowhere.

But it is late, isn't it.

Yes. I went for a drink, he said.

No, he hadn't told her.

He went to the cupboard for a glass. She was close to him, leaning towards him like a dog. He had forgotten his jacket. It was in the car. He said he'd be just a moment.

From outside he looked back towards the house, through the window of the living room and could see her in the lamplight; sitting on the couch and waiting for him.

It was later that night I found him. He was curled up at the bottom of the bed holding my right foot. There was moon on him and just the two of us, curled like a comma and the letter C. I took my foot from his hands and crawled down to him.

He had reached over earlier in the night and put his hand on my hip. I had moved away.

Why do you do that? he said.

What.

That.

I don't.

I could no longer let him touch me. I could not stand the feeling that his body would always want something from me. He said it was not the case, that he did not expect anything. But how could he not.

And I wonder now, as I did then, what that world was that I found myself in with him. One that we did not clearly refuse, and so our acceptance was assumed.

It was early morning when I woke to find him standing beside the bed in wet boots and holding a bucket towards me.

The water has frozen, he said, it's that cold. With the frost and the ice thick on the windscreen. I pulled myself up. Outside there was white sunlight. Look, he said. I looked and reached over to touch the thin ice in the bucket. Careful, my mother would say, careful. Ah, I said, drawing my hand back, it's cold.

Of course it's cold, he laughed.

What did you bring it here for?

To show you. You should come out, there's frost. The grass yellow and burnt by the cold. Come on, he said. I'll carry you. No, I said, I'd like to walk.

My mother arrived then, I heard her. He went outside to meet her and I could hear them talking. I looked out the window. She came into my room and said that it was time for a walk. She tied her laces in a double bow and looked for the dog lead. She said she didn't understand how we could live there, in all that grey. Come on, she said, hurry up, I told you ten minutes ago. She had not. She had only just arrived. She said she had called out to me from the bottom of the stairs, that I must have heard her.

I forgot, I said.

He is coming, she said. He is waiting – no, here he comes now, I can hear him.

Are we going? he asked. He was at the door.

I thought we were going to see the frost, I said.

What frost? my mother replied. Come on, we're waiting for you.

Oh.

Give me those pyjamas and I'll wash them. This room smells, she said.

I can't smell anything.

He turned to the window while I changed. Mother stood there with her hand out, I put my clothes into them. That's the girl, she said. Hurry up then.

There was music. What's that noise? she asked.

It's music.

From where?

Next door.

That woman, I suppose. My mother had seen Isabel and did not like her.

Yes, probably.

In my room I could smell nasturtium flowers wilting. He had picked them and put them in a bottle, but when they fade they burn. They shrivel up with all the acid. They're good for horses someone once told me, the leaves.

Can you smell them? I asked. But she was not listening.

He bent down to tie my shoes. He said, it's nice out. You can smell wood smoke. He knows how I like wood smoke.

We went outside. It was nice out, they were right, the air was good in my chest, light. But it was cold there in the morning, before the sun was in the yard, and soon we went back in. Mother stayed a while and he went to work. Shortly after she too left. That day she could not stay long. After a while there were many days when she could not stay long.

It is the following morning and the movie people have not returned. It is early still, the sun hasn't yet made its way down the buildings and into the street. Maybe, I think, they will come later in the afternoon. Already, though, there are people from the apartment block sitting on their front steps, waiting for the movie star to arrive.

I waited.

Isabel came in the afternoon and made me tea. She took me outside and sat with me in the garden. She had her hair out. She had her arms open and stretched them along the back of the chair. She was wearing something which smelled like green apples, and underneath that something chemical. As though her freshness was lying. There was sunlight and leaf shadow on her. Across from us, in the house hidden behind the row of mandarin trees, a man played some lazy chord over and over while we drank bitter tea thick with milk. It left a scum line on the inside of the cup which I saw her wipe away with her fingers. She closed her eyes. There was blue beneath them. You are tired, I said. Yes. Her feet hurt. Leave, I said. I knew that she did not like her job. I had heard her return home late the night before, heard her drop her keys, swear and unlock her house. Her phone rang. Who would know she had arrived home? Someone. She didn't say. Men in suits, she said. She can't tell, it's dark in there. They're all the same. Like foreigners. Germans. Asians. English. What's the difference. Ooh la la, she said. Ooh la la. But when she said it, it did not sound anything like how I had heard it said in the movies.

But she said, no. It's money. I know that, I replied.

It is strange the way you remember your life first thing in the morning. The way you forget your life first thing in the morning and then you remember it. Years ago I would wake up and forget and then remember – that he was in my world – and I would smile to myself because he was there and it was such a good thing to remember then.

Later I would wake up and forget, and then remember that waking meant it was morning which meant that I had a whole day to go before I could return to sleep and when I woke after that there would be another day and another day all over again.

Now I wake and both forget and remember so many different things. I remember everything and sometimes I remember so much that I do not know what to do with it and so I go back to sleep.

I saw a man in a brown jacket early this morning and I thought for a moment that it was him. He was coming down the steps of a building and doing up his buttons against the cold. I came back to the hotel and phoned his number. I did not think about it. I did not think anything. It rang, a woman answered and I hung up. I phoned again and a man answered although it was not him. Hello, I said. He could not hear me. Hello, he said. Hello, I said again. It was his father. The woman had been his mother and not a lover. I asked to speak to him. He is in sleep still, his father said. He is in sleep. I had not thought of someone being in sleep before, as though it were a particular place one entered into and remained. Don't bother him then, I said, I can phone back later, although I knew that I wouldn't. No, he said, it is late and about time he was up. I heard him put the receiver down on the table and go to wake his son. I put the phone back on the hook and did not call again.

He had a history of falling in love with mad women – with fragile women, with strong women who had become weak. One of them tried to kill him once by threatening him with a baseball bat and she would have done it, he said, had he not jumped out a window and ran. She had what it took to kill a man, he said.

He liked women who needed him and whom he could care for. He had been brought up to believe that was what one must do. But inevitably they did not continue to appreciate his care and he could not continue to empathise and we began to resent each other because of the very thing he continued offering, the very thing I wished I did not need to receive.

I miss you when you are not here, I said to him as he prepared for work, showering and buttoning a clean shirt before realising that he had forgotten to shave.

You should not miss me, he said, taking off his shirt and running water into the white basin.

But I do.

It was the truth and it was also a lie. I did miss him, my days were lonely. But despite my expectations, seeing him at the end of the day did not make me happy as it once had.

You should not miss me, he said, watching his reflection in the mirror as he drew the razor up his neck. He did not want to be missed. And I could tell by the way he dressed, pulling his shirt on in a hurry with his back bent over, as he had not unbuttoned it, and by the way he quickly said goodbye, that he no longer missed me.

That evening he brought home fish for dinner. He unwrapped it from its paper and placed it in the sink. What have you got? I asked. You'll see. He ran water over the fish and flicked off a few remaining scales. I went to sit down while he chopped onions and herbs and garlic. There was the rattle of the fry pan and hot oil. Above it the radio played and he called out that it was almost ready. I was in the living room. He called to me again. Coming, I said but he didn't hear me. He called again as I entered the kitchen. It smells lovely, I said. He served the fish onto plates and took it to the table. I thanked him and picked at it a little, but didn't eat. Are you not hungry? he asked. No, I said, I can't eat this. You know I can't eat this.

What do you mean? He stopped eating and sat still, holding his knife and fork. We used to eat fish all the time, he said.

Vegetables are fine, I answered.

Well, he said, the cat will like it, and that next time he won't bother in fact he does not know why he bothers, bothers with any of this, that it has all become ridiculous. He was standing then, he had taken both our plates and was scraping the food into the garbage bin. He said that he did not know what was wrong with me, why no one knew what it was that was wrong with me and maybe it was nothing and maybe if I ate something decent I would get strong, and that I should get out and do something. I am sick, he said, I am sick of doing everything.

I left then. I got up from the table and went to my room; he was still yelling behind me as he threw the clean cutlery into a drawer. I shut the door.

He was sitting quietly at the table when I returned to the kitchen for a glass of water. He didn't look at me when I entered and I walked straight past him. I remembered that same posture, that dark sulkiness that I had recognised when we were first together in the city by the harbour. I should have paid more attention to that moment, I thought. I remembered at the time thinking that I should remember it, for it seemed to happen with every lover – that initial moment, sometimes before we had even spoken, when I could foretell everything about them which, years later, I might find possible to hate. Arrogance, or this suggestion in their posture that they have a tendency to sulk. I feared greatly the prospect of living with a man in this state, silent and brooding and sharp at the edges.

I was filling my glass with water when he opened his mouth to speak. Before he had made a sound I was already hoping that he would say something I might love and which might discredit the logic of my fears. He spoke. But the tap was running and I did not hear him. What did you say? I asked, but he would not repeat himself.

Nothing, he said. There is nothing wrong.

Sickness borrowed my body as I now borrow him. We took from each other everything that we could and gave back what we had left. I was using him. He knew this. Even though I loved him. Of course I loved him. But I knew that I was not offering, and could not offer him – anything. I was consumed by my own body even as it was diminishing.

And I borrow him now even though he has gone. I have stolen him, I have stolen those years that we shared and kept them. And I can understand how a woman might be driven to murder. I can understand how that strange mixture of hate and longing, that desire both to have someone and lose them completely, might come about.

He used to say that everyone is mad once you know them well enough, and that it is both madness to marry a person and madness not to. He would say that insanity is quite an ordinary thing between two people once they have lived together for any significant period of time.

It is Monday today. There is still no movie shooting. It has been three days and the movie crew has not come back.

Tuesday. And no movie. Of course there is no movie. They will not be back. It seems they only wanted the steps and three strides of the street.

***

He asked for a photo of me once but I did not have one. Or rather, I had many but none that was the self he knew and that I could give to him. This was when we did not see each other every day and he wanted something to remember me by when I was not with him, like the lovers and the photographer I saw in the city taking photographs of each other in the park. It was a sunny day when I saw them. There were couples sitting in the rose garden and children with ice-creams. The young lovers had a number of photos taken together and then they posed separately, him with one leg up on a step and his elbow resting on his knee and she standing alone in long black pants and high heels with her hands on her hips. I never know whether to be impressed or horrified by people who can pose like that, and they did it again and again and again until the light changed and the sun slipped down behind the trees. They left then, holding hands. I watched him pull her close and slide one hand into the back pocket of her pants. The photographer packed up his cameras and headed off in the opposite direction.

It was evening and the pigeons started to rustle about, looking for somewhere warm to go. They are everywhere in this city but I have not seen people feeding them. People don't often feed pigeons here, only seagulls. They are scruffy-looking pigeons, many with no feathers left about their necks, and on the bus going home I saw some trying to find shelter in a church window. One was perched on the gold cross that was attached to the noticeboard publicising the services for the week, while behind this, in the alcove of the window, two birds shuffled about. They could have been fighting or mating, I could not tell, for one was perched on top of the other, moving about, and I could see its dusty wings opening and twisting and opening and twisting as it worked its body into the small space of the window ledge and every now and then you could see the head or the wing of the bird beneath and then there would again be the opening and the twisting as they moved quickly, impatiently – city birds they were, quite clearly – the head of the one on top pushing down on the bird beneath and then the two of them lifting their wings without taking flight and twisting until it looked as though their wings would break. They were not comfortable. A cold wind had come up and they had very little space to share. With the bus stopped in traffic I watched them until at last the bird on top lifted its grey wing and, opening it out, laid it over the bird beneath.

What are you doing? he said.

Nothing. I had the newspaper open and was drawing over it with a pencil.

Do you want to do anything? His voice.

No, as something like pigeons took off in my head again. These creatures, lying there sleeping with the darkness over them and their wings folded over one another and then something, someone, throws a stone at them, in there (what are you doing? he's saying. What?) and they rise up, all their feathers and bones in the small container of air they are kept in, the size of a head, and they beat about, their small beaks opening and their thin tongues–

Would you stop that please.

I think no.

Please.

No.

My father taught me how to draw like this, to take a pen and begin a line, anywhere on the page, it does not matter, and draw the line all over itself, keep going, fill the whole page if you like. But don't lift the pen off. You must remember: the thing is to make certain that no one can see where the line begins and where it ends.

I'd like to read that, he said. (It is the back page. It has the crosswords on it. He never does the crosswords.)

And then when the line meets up with itself, somewhere, you colour in the spaces. Not all the spaces. Just some.

The paper built wings then and flew.

I said stop, he said. He had made it fly. He had pulled it out from under me. I stopped.

The birds snapped quiet. The wings I had heard lifting to the top of my head were clipped. It was a quick sound, a thin echo of metal snapping through feathers and hollow bone.

He made me stop. He said I scared him, that a person shouldn't do the things that I did, bending down and scribbling like a child. The birds came down. They did not fly up again. Half-winged things that could not make it over the fence of my head.

Why don't you just read it, he said.

It is boring.

He knows that I do not read it because I can't. I do not read anything any more.

You always make a mess of the paper, he said. He said he doesn't know how I do it and that after I have looked at it he can never fit it back together. I'm sorry. I don't know how I do it, I said.

I'll get you white paper if you want.

No. I'm fine.

Good, he said, and took the newspaper away.

And I could hear them shuffling. Dragging their blunt wings about. They missed the sunlight. I turned my ear to the sky. To let it in.

In my hotel room my bed is beside a window that looks out over a brick wall and across to a church. When I wake late into the night I can gaze into the wall as though it were the darkness of the night because there is never real night darkness here.

Last night I dreamed that I was talking to him and telling him of these dreams I had been having about him. I told him as though it were a strange thing that I should have had these dreams, as though he were absent, when here he was. And the dreams that I told him were presented exactly as they happened, perfectly reproduced by my recounting, and it did not occur to me while I was telling him and remembering them that I was myself still dreaming. It was a first-hand dream and a second-hand dream at the same time, moving both backwards and forwards, for nothing happened in it except for his presence, the whole thing was about his presence, and how strange it was that I should have ever dreamed that he was gone.

Things remained as they were, we could do nothing to alter them. The seasons passed, it was summer and the Agapanthus opened by halves in the dark. We had been waiting for them, the flowers. My mother called them pregnant. We watched them let go of their green leaves, then their petals. I have an aunt who is fond of these. The same one who wears her heart on her sleeve. She ties the flowers by their long necks with string and hangs them upside down in a dark closet to dry. She says they are lovely at weddings.

Inside each flower there is a well. Once I knew the names for all the inside parts: the organs and the liquids, the gold dust, like an old word – illness, it is like a flower – thin and yellow, flattened in a book and forgotten. The others say the word sick, and I look out the window into the valley, trying not to listen to them. It is like a well, the valley, this illness, something that lies itself down inside a shadow.

But I can hear them talking about me. They are in the kitchen. They use the word sick because it is less insidious, shorter, a nauseating but brief discomfort. And then it passes. While illness is a flower. I am a thin-stemmed floral-headed thing. Like the African violets clambering in scraps of dirt now that the sun has come.

No one said what the sickness was. Nothing can be proven and a name lasts. A word for something comes to live in you, you own each other, your name, the name of the thing you're sharing. Words become you. It is raggedness that sits on my tongue amongst the bird calls now. For there are too many pieces of my mouth to make it speak, while I watch water shadow, how it comes, moves across the wall. Sunlight in the glass I was drinking from. It stops. Moves again.

His hands, one white, one white again, move through his dark hair and his light eyes, green, sometimes grey, look to the ceiling. I hear him breathing. In, and then he doesn't breathe out again. He is looking at the patches where the paint is peeling. But the ceiling doesn't give him what he wants and he comes back to me. Mother has gone now. All his breath goes out then and his hands come away from his head. His legs are crossed. I can see the leg on top pulsing as his blood moves and the shadow of his nipple beneath his light blue shirt. He has been at work. Beside him on the table is a glass of gin. There is, for some reason, no lemon in it. He drinks it without speaking. I ask him how his day was. Good, he said. He ate lunch in the sun and watched the men play chess in Hyde Park. It is always the man who looks least likely to win who wins, he said. I like Hyde Park. The sunlight and the water and the birds, people on park benches. I can hear him chewing on the ice cubes. They make a low clinking in the glass at first which gets higher and higher as they shrink and then he eats them.

He is quiet then. The light leaves the room and I saw words fall from him. Like old skin without being spoken. I did not know what they were but I knew they were there. I heard them hit the ground. I could taste their dust and their dull shape.

Outside, the woman in the blue raincoat walks along the road collecting the daily papers that had been thrown into front yards. She does this every week, filling bag after bag with papers and taking them home.

He undoes the top buttons of his shirt then, and moves once from his chair to kiss me. He touches my hair. He says, it will be alright. Don't you worry, you'll see. And I trust him.

Isabel had come with clean sheets that morning and fruit. I had sat in the chair and watched her change my bed for me, tossing the old sheets into a pile and throwing on the new. The white billowed as she shook it out in front of her – the white sheet then the light – the sun coming above the ridge and striking through the window, hitting the wall above her head like a bird against clean glass and falling, spreading its life slowly through the room until time takes it, tucking it into hours, her, tucking the corners of the sheets under the mattress and folding the top sheet down. There is nothing like clean sheets, she said, and then, there you are. She said, come on, let's get you something to eat.

We went into the kitchen and she took two white bowls from the cupboard. She had brought pawpaw and watermelon. She sliced the pawpaw in half and scooped the seeds out into one bowl. Then sliced the fruit and, taking it from its skin, placed the cut pieces in the other. She took a lemon from the fruit bowl, sliced it in half and squeezed it with her hands over the fruit. Then she put both hands in the bowl and turned the fruit over itself so that it was all coated with lemon and carried it to the table outside. I followed her, bringing the watermelon and a knife.

We ate the pawpaw with our fingers, the watermelon too. Later she went to the sink to wash her hands so as not to eat more but when I asked, she said that she had had her more already, and the juice that had collected in the shell of the watermelon dripped slowly between the cracks of the wooden table and onto the ground.

Then she took me by the arm, above the elbow, gently, the way you are taught to lead the blind, and walked me down to the lake.

Above him the clock ticked on the living room wall. Night was still coming. It was a long day and at the same time felt later than I had expected. We both looked at the clock, him having to uncross his legs and turn around. We had been listening to it ticking until finally we had to look. He asked me if I had taken my afternoon sleep. I said, Isabel doesn't ask that, I said, Isabel says poor thing. That's what your mother says, he said, getting up and going towards the kitchen for another drink, and you hate it. That is different. Why? Because she is my mother and I am not talking about my mother now. He said that last time my mother said that, I told her to be quiet. I told her that I was not a dog, because that is how she talks to dogs and to small children, with music and quietness instead of words.

Isabel says everything you need, he said. And I said, yes.

She took me to the lake and we removed our shoes and walked, very carefully, holding each other for balance in the mud and we did not have to speak. She looked for stones and when she found a good heavy one she would clean it off and hurl it as far as she could into the water. We would wait then, for the sound of its splash, like waiting for the gap between thunder and lightning. How close, how far is our danger. Throwing the stones away from us and listening to them break the surface, to the birds on the other side lifting up and calling and moving away.

I followed him to the kitchen where he took off his tie, the red and blue striped one that I had chosen for him that morning. He had five to choose from. Which one? he had asked, and I had pointed, and he had accepted it although I knew it was not his favourite. You have five, I'd say, you can not wear your favourite every day. Unbuttoning his sleeve now, and pushing back his hair (always pushing back his hair), opening the cupboard taking the bottle pouring another drink, always pouring a drink, – it is his evening, it is his time, what he chooses to do with it. Lemon? he asked. Do we have a lemon? He could not find it before. Yes, I said, in the fridge. In the cold, as she was – in the water – when she called, come in, while I hovered in the shade, sweat itching my face. I followed her in and once I was in the water she chased me. I could not go fast enough to escape, with the effort of pushing myself through water and without the sureness of being able to see what lay beneath the surface. For there were sharp things on the ground, stones and maybe glass thrown in by the young boys heard down there yelling out late at night and jumping into the cold water from a rope tied to a tree. The water was cold and she was throwing it, picking it up in her hands and throwing it away. To have empty things, you can't empty it; and then she was throwing it at me and running around me and I was caught in the middle as she worked the water into a small whirlpool and threw herself in and pulled me down with her and we drifted.

It's easier for her, he said, standing with his back to me at the kitchen bench. As if it were hardest for him, I thought. And what about me, I said. What about you? It is all you, I am all you, everyone loves you, he said. I love you, loved you, she didn't even know you then. I looked at him. I love you too, I said.

I only want you well, he said, turning to me, still holding the lemon and the knife. I went silent then. He said my name. Yes? I replied. He was checking to make sure I was listening. Yes? I said. Nothing. What? Nothing, he said.

Out of the water the ground was hot underneath us and she lay beside me and I could feel parts of her body close to me, like familiar music heard through a wall, and we spoke about our sorrows, about how near or far our passion felt from our skin. So far some days.

Blood is not family, he used to tell me. Family can be anyone you choose to love. I agreed, but said also that family are the people you are stuck with. You have your family for life and even after that. Even if you abandon them you still belong; even if you try to forget them, you will remember. We were a family, he said. Just the two of us. We did not need her, he said.

When I was a teenager it was fashionable to be stricken by grief, to be unusual in that way. People paid attention to you and they talked about you. Everybody wanted to know what was wrong, and would compete as to who knew you the best, who most understood the particularities of your sadness.

The two of them became like this. Rivalling one another, he to lay claim to me as his loved burden, she to prove that she knew how to care for me best. They pretended, though, that it had nothing to do with such competition and that it was a basic matter of dislike and dissimilarity between them.

What would she know about the real world? he said. What would she know about caring for you? What would you know, what would – the two of us – he was thinking of the two of us together when he was at work and how much time we wasted in a day. He presumed he knew the world and its real ways because he worked in it. He forgot that he didn't used to, and that his aim was never to have to.

Do you really think, I said, that the rest of the world matters to me? I do not belong there; I do not think many people do, I said. Even he was pretending. He knew that most of us live somewhere altogether else, and outside of us is another place that we call the Real World and sometimes we visit, and sometimes we tell ourselves that that is where we live.

I still watched it though, the world, and remembered when he had done the same – examining long afternoon shadows and the sunlight. Fruit, and water reflected on the white ceiling. We once shared a way of conceiving the real world differently, as though the two of us, in the way two people together do, had fashioned a world unique and new.

This was what I saw, and he too had once noticed these things. It had been in his painterly interest. And for a time I provided these sights as the day's significant details and he had been attentive. He would come home and I would tell him about the importance of what might otherwise be considered unimportant things. But by that time, inside – in the second bedroom which he had once used as a studio – old canvases lay stacked against the wall and dust had settled on his paper. He did not want to go in there. Why? I asked. He said that he had nothing to say. I told him he was looking at the world the wrong way, that he knew it was not about saying anything as such, and that of course he would have nothing to say, no one does, and that by way of saying, as he knew, you only say what you realise you did not mean to say at all. He looked at me, taking me in – as he did – and, returning the lemon to the fridge, walked away.

Mother came the next day. She brought red meat for me and dinner for the dog. Blood she said, it was blood I needed. I heard her let herself in and begin to prepare the food in the kitchen. She was quiet, afraid of waking me. But I was not sleeping, I rarely slept then, it had become impossible even though I was exhausted.

She had a smell, my mother, underneath her violet water perfume; a hot smell of fried mince and onions and a cold smell of congealed meat fat. Today she would begin with the hot smell, as I could hear her, downstairs chopping onions, and knew that her tongue would be pushing against the inside of her cheek as she cut at them hard with a blunt knife. It was best that she did this early. She didn't like me in the kitchen with her, watching. My vacant eyes, she thought, measuring her uneven slices of vegetable, wanting to tell her that it could be done differently – that there is a pattern to slicing an onion so that all its pieces separate.

Didn't anyone teach you that at school? I asked her one night. No. I couldn't help it though – I had to tell her the other way to cut onions: halve, quarter lengthways, and then cut across. She pushed the knife down diagonally, and said you're just like your father. I could have said that I did not know enough of him to argue against this but I didn't. I just said that I found it easier that way and left her. I could have said that my father did not teach me anything about onions, that I have no recollection of either of them cooking when I was a child.

She sighed. I could hear it above the spitting of the meat fat. I hated the sound of her sighing. I hated it that she thought no one else noticed, and that she never said what it was that saddened or bothered her. Some great weight that she wished she could be rid of – the thought of the possible length of the day. I know that.

But it might not be that at all. It might simply be that she was trained to be a singer and was taught to release her breath. Letting out the stale air of night and its silences, its rowdy dreams and all the things that we leave unspoken.

The dog's bowl scraped on the floor as it shoved its nose so far into the food that it pushed it away from itself. I heard her speak to it, that's the girl, she said, that's the girl, as she came upstairs to see me. She had brought me fresh clothes and stayed in the room while I dressed. She did not need to do this, I said, I was not that weak. My body, she said, for she was watching me although she pretended not to, was like it was as a girl – skinny and brittle. So this is it, I think, this is what it is, all this, me, becoming again a child.

You are just like your father she had said to me, even as a girl, and I remember her saying once that my father was like a lizard. This was when they were still together, when we all mistook habit for love. A snake, another voice said, he reminds me of a slimy snake. There was a group of them, my mother's singing ladies, downstairs drinking tea and gnawing at my mother's burnt fruitcake. Yes, said my mother, a slimy snake, while all the time I had privately prided myself in my likeness to her. But there is little of me now that resembles her the way I once did, the way I was born with the muscle of her calves. It had not occurred to my parents that one could inherit muscle, but my mother said later that of course she knew because I had been a ferocious kicker whilst inside her. I took pride in myself that this was our likeness. It was not complicated, it was not deep. It meant that I could walk and dance like she did, and it had nothing to do with temper or melancholy or impatience. It did not occur to anyone that I had inherited her face, thus inheriting the complexities that hid behind it and the confused ways in which men had loved it and the ways by which that love had been returned. It had been, before, a simple matter of physical strength, this was what we had always shared. And this was what left me, withering away like some strange skin so that we no longer knew in what ways we resembled one another, so that it became impossible to locate ourselves by the likeness of our bodies. So that often I would look at her then and she would appear to me a stranger.

There were two things my father said to me, both more to himself than to me, but I heard them and remembered them. He said, the guilt of leaving someone you love never goes away. And, he said, never try to argue with a mad woman.

So although my mother was with me we did not speak about my father. She said that I was like him and that was all. Besides, it was not as though I was dying, at least not in the near future, and so there was no reason for us to confess and make peace quickly. No; my days, the prospect of the rest of my life, seemed long enough as it was.

Mother cooked my meals but did not stay the night, she did not like to stay the night, leaving instead when I went to sleep. I woke to hear Isabel entering the house early the next morning. She did not knock, just walked in, for we rarely locked the house and she assumed, rightly I suppose (although it surprised me), that she could enter. He had gone some hours before and I was still in bed.

She came into my room. She looked at me and said she thought it time I washed my hair. I agreed. I had forgotten about my hair, although I had showered. It took such an effort to lift my hands to my head and then to have to rub and rinse and keep the soap from falling into my eyes. Would you like me to wash it for you? she asked. Yes, I said, please.

Is there a bucket, a tub, something I can fill with water?

Yes, in the laundry.

She went then. I could hear her running the taps, I imagined her checking the temperature of the water with the inside of her wrist. Then I heard her coming up the stairs, slowly, so the water would not spill.

She sat on the end of the bed and put the blue tub on the chest of drawers beside me. She put a towel on my lap and wrapped another around my shoulders and across my neck. Her fingers brushed my skin a moment, by accident. They were light, warm. She didn't ask me how it was that we should do it. Just lifted the tub and rested it in my lap on top of the towel. I was sitting up and the tub of water rested quite safely between the blankets. There was a washer floating in it and she had brought a cup.

Bend your head over, she said, and my hair fell over my face, its ends just touching the water. She dipped the cup into the bucket and, lifting it, emptied it slowly across my head. The warmth seeped through my hair, into my scalp and slipped off the front of my forehead and back into the tub.

The back of my head was wet. Isabel cupped her hand to my hairline above my temple. She poured more water and it ran down the side of my face towards my ear, making it wet inside. A few drops hit the water. There, she said, and took her hand away. She opened the bottle of shampoo and poured some into her palm. My head was still down but from the corner of my eye I could see her. She had poured out a circle of shampoo the size of a twenty cent piece and she rubbed this into my head. It smelled of flowers, imitation flowers, I could not tell which ones. Bouquet it would be called, Floral Bouquet.

Bend your head again, she said. And took the cup and scooped up water. She placed it beside the bed and squeezed out the washer. Here, she said, folding it over in three, hold this against your eyes. I did. It was warm and dark and I could see the blood behind my closed eyes and feel the water pouring again across my head, rinsing off the shampoo and falling back, rinsing off and falling back. I did not ever want it to stop.

She pulled the towel up higher on the back of my neck so that I did not get cold, but I could feel that the water was cooling. And my back began to ache a little from bending. Then she said, there you are, it's done now. And I said, thank you. She took the towel from my neck and wrapped my hair in it. You are not cold? she asked. No, thank you, I said again.

Outside there was the sound of kookaburras. She said that it would rain. She was standing then, taking the tub from my lap. It feels like there will be rain, she said, you can smell it. She dropped the washer and the cup into the tub and went out, returning some minutes later to help me lie down. She told me I should try to sleep and that she would be back in the afternoon. You don't have to, I said, but she knew this. She said she'd like to. When's he coming home? she asked. I don't know. Sometime. He said he'd be home sometime. She nodded, hovered a moment, then bent and kissed me on the cheek before she left.

In between we became almost terrible to one another. Is this what we are all about? he said, this time desperate. Is it? Love he meant. We were sitting at the kitchen table with the night over us and the fridge behind us, humming and clicking off and humming, and I said, no, I said that we did not have to make it that way, as if there were a choice. Life is what you make it, his father said to him, while my mother told me that sometimes it is just what you're given, and as often as we could we would try to forget all this and we would try to be kind, look gently at each other across the table. Him twisting his glass around and around, how he always twisted his glass with one hand and touched my arm with the other, and once he had twisted out whatever needed to be twisted he'd take his hand off the glass and place it, too, on my arm, holding me with one warm hand and one cold.

That night was different though. Kindness at the table did not change things. There was streetlight in our cream room as I lay awake. Outside it was raining heavily and there was a steady swish of cars passing along the highway. I lay there, listening, wondering where they were all going and why there were so many of them, for it sounded like a procession, on and on, swish and swish swish, until I turned over and realised that it was him and his breathing.

It was past two in the morning and I had been awake since we went to bed, since he had suggested, not long after we had eaten, that we go to bed and talk a little. He had only just put his head on the pillow when he fell asleep. I hated this – him falling asleep before me and leaving me stranded in my own wakefulness, sharing neither his company nor my own.

I got up and went to the window but could hear him breathing even from the other side of the room.

The next night I would not let him go to sleep without me and so I lay on top of him in the dark and talked and talked and talked at him until he said he felt sick with the need for sleep, until he was speaking to me in both dream language and waking language, until he was coming out with insensible things and not knowing he had said them, and when, still on top of him, I answered his questions he accused me of waking him and swore that he had not said a thing.

I go about my days now crossing streets, buying food, catching the bus. These things happen to me, these things are what I do. These minor things that fill most of my life. And I do these things neither in another's company nor in my own, but between things, between tasks and between people, between myself and those closest to me. Every now and then, though, I am stunned out of this; it is as though life catches up with me, or I with it, and I am cut to the quick with a memory that feels too close ever to be remembered.

My heart is breaking, he said once. My heart is breaking. And I wondered later what the heart is made from if one can narrate its process of decay and not just say that, like a dropped glass, it has broken. For this is what it is, broken and breaking, a remembering and a forgetting all at once. The way that today, for a moment, I forgot him and I forgot illness and I forgot everything this city now reminds me of. And then remembered. I was in a second-hand shop, looking at old dresses and shoes that I might buy and would probably never wear, picking up pieces, holding a jacket up to myself before a mirror, and it came at me – everything all at once, him, the city, illness all over – and I put the jacket down, picked up my bag and walked back onto the street. We do not get over anything. It becomes, over time, less acute, but it comes back, it always comes back, hitting me hard in the chest when I least expect it and never quite making it to that tame place that is known to us as memory.

I walked out onto the street and headed downtown, although not thinking that it was downtown, towards the markets. I had forgotten if they were on this day, had forgotten what day it was anyway, but I was certain they would be on, although when I arrived at the place where I expected to find them they were not there. I walked around the square and came back to where I thought I had started from, and sure enough they were there, where I had expected them to be. What was it that I had not seen? Boxes of apples and bread. Carts of vegetables and flowers. There were pots of yellow marigolds lined up on the ground and a man rushing past me, knocking me with a package he was carrying and someone else telling me to watch where I was going, lady. Lady. I had not bumped into them, I was not even about to, but I had sunglasses on and although they were dark they were not dark enough to completely hide my eyes and it was quite clear to anyone who looked that I was quite vacant. I passed the corner I was sure I had only just encountered, crossing paths with a woman I had seen only a moment before, as though I was walking in circles, and yet I was not. I no longer knew which way I had come from or which way to go. I had entirely forgotten what it was that I had come to buy, and why I would buy anything anyway seeing that I ate all my food in the hotel and my room had nothing to cook with. But I had come to buy something. I recalled – tomatoes. And flowers, flowers for my room. I found the tomatoes, I found four different types and bought one of each. I held out my bag of tomatoes for the man and he took it from my hands and weighed them. He called a price and I paid him. He had blue eyes and a hat to match. He smiled at me. I did not know what to do with this. Have a nice afternoon, he said.

There is something comforting about the city in grief. The way it distracts you and offers you company that does not intrude. I can speak or not as I choose, pick things up and put them down again. I need not buy anything. There is nothing that I must take possession of while at the same time everything offers itself. Here I am not responsible for anything, not even the weight and movement of my own thoughts. And I can be with anyone I choose just by imagining what I would buy for them if I could, what it might be that I would give.

This is what I did after him. I moved to the city. I took to staying up late into the night and drinking wine. I took to doing all the things that we once did together, before I was ill, and which he had always said he should try to give up. I no longer needed to sleep or eat as I once did. I did the work that I needed to do during the day and then at night I would go out. I wore my coat, I carried my keys. I imagined all the things that someone might do to me should they attack me and all the ways I would try and fight back. And I thought of him, and I thought of other things. Strange, that I should feel so at ease, walking in the night while considering so much violence.

In the night the house smelled of his cigarettes. It was still raining and he had been smoking inside. Outside a wind picked up, and it came in because I had to have the windows open to let out the stale smell. The tap in the bathroom dripped. In the distance was a siren. Fire, ambulance, police, I have never been certain of their differences – what particular state of emergency it is that we are caught within.

It did not get any easier. I went to buy milk one night from the shop on the corner, and approaching the house on my return, I kept walking, slowly, thinking that if I did everything would resolve.

When I came back he was outside, talking on the phone. I imagined he would not be on the phone long and so I waited. But he kept going, when he knew I was home. So I sat and waited more. I could not hear what he was saying through the thickness of the glass door and when he came in I didn't ask. He asked me what was on my mind and I said, nothing. I said, I don't know. I said nothing.

I did not walk as far as I would have liked to; I would have liked to walk all the way along the back streets, if we were in the city I would have walked to the harbour, but I didn't, I couldn't, and besides, he would have worried about where I had gone. That was his job now, he had said. He had said, in the nicest of ways, that from now on he would worry about me, he would care.

They had met in the city, at a gallery where his work was on display. She came across him outside, smoking a cigarette.

I like your work, she said to him. He stubbed out the cigarette and tried to light another, sheltering by the wall. There was some pause before his reply; thank you, he said, his voice muffled by smoke.

She didn't understand it but it was one of those odd things that she felt she could live with, as if it was already known. She said this and he asked her if she painted.

No, she said, she told him that she did a bit of teaching, but that she was a dancer really, that she'd always wanted to be a singer, that her mother was a singer, that she – no, her mother was not really a singer, but she had always wanted to be one too.

At that point she swallowed the rest of her wine. She had no idea why she was telling him those things. She thought it must be his silence, that silent men always seemed to make her talk. But he appeared to be listening, nodding. He is too polite, she thought, he must be accustomed to this, admiring women chatting to the man whom they mistake for the work.

A singer? he asked, and she looked at him. Yes.

I'd love to sing, he said.

No, you wouldn't, it's annoying really, once you begin it is impossible to stop. He smiled at this, he said that those were the only things worth doing.

The next night he painted her. That isn't me, she said, when he showed it to her.

It is, he replied.

It looks nothing like me. She recognised only her clothes, her black shoes with a shine on them, her red dress. She turned away from it and moved towards the kitchen. He followed her. No, he said, conceding, you are right, it looks nothing like you. She was opening and closing cupboards. Why is it, she asked loudly, that you do not have any food here?

Quiet–

Why?

It's late.

I'm hungry, she said. He was sorry, he had not anticipated her coming. He should have thought ahead, she said. You should know that I am always hungry.

I think now of every lost moment with you. Of every kindness we did not grant. When you offered something that might have eased things and I refused. Come on, you said, when you came home to find me one night weeping on the kitchen floor because you were late when you had said you would not be. Come on, you said, let's go for a drive, let's go out. I refused and you didn't argue. I wish that I had said yes. I wish that we had driven out into the dark, stopped somewhere, got out and stood at the side of some empty street, some clearing. I wonder now what it was we might have said. Those words, gone now.

Come to bed then, you said, come to bed and we'll talk. But only moments after we had turned out the light you were asleep again and we had said nothing.

The next day I spent the morning with Isabel, even though he was home. From where we sat in her kitchen we could hear the steady fall of the axe as he split the last lot of wood left over from winter.

He was chopping wood only the other week, she said. Yes, I answered.

We sat, warming our hands around teacups, while outside the axe cut at the air. I knew he did not like me seeing her. He was always worried it would tire me, everything, that everything might tire me. That was his excuse. But I did not tell her this. I knew it was jealousy. Her chair squeaked on the floor as she pushed it back from the table. The kettle was boiling and its steam fogged the window. I could hear that his axe had stopped and could see the small dark blur of him moving about on the other side of the glass, bending and carrying. She saw me watching him and leaning forward, reached across the table for my arm.

It rained again today when I was out walking. It poured so hard that the whole city retreated. I had only a small umbrella and it turned up in the wind. Ahead of me was a church and I went into it to escape the weather. Others had gathered there too, but under the awning, still outside. I went in. It was cold and there was a smell of wood polish. I sat down at the back. Before me a man knelt in supplication – praying so hard that I could see his shoulders shake.

On my own in the city I no longer speak.

We fooled ourselves with an intimacy; eventually, eventually we were only fooling ourselves. We killed it. While I try to hold my whole world open now, as though everything might be returned to.

In the narrow space between my hotel and the church next door a man on the ground is singing and late at night I hear bells ring out across the city. But I myself have become dumb; looking for someone and speaking to a man I know I will never see – like a statue of a woman whose lips are open while her mouth remains filled with stone.

She took my face in one hand and pulled herself towards it. Let's fix this up, she said. She had a bag of make-up and she tipped it out across the bed. She had all the colours. What are your favourites? Blue, and red. You have dark eyes, she said. Blue wouldn't suit them. She flicked through the other colours. But if you really want.

He wore make-up once, he told me. Mascara. When he was a guitarist in a band.

Close, Isabel said. I closed. And open. She wore a loose singlet and when she said open I opened and I could see down her top to her breasts hanging like two small teats of a cow while she held onto my face, checking one eye against the other to make sure she had painted them evenly. Close again, she said. I closed. I could feel her breathing on my face. I had a dentist once who always ate peanut butter sandwiches for lunch. I knew this because he bent over me like she did and I could smell him too. And open.

Next we do your lips. Like this, she said, sucking her lips over her teeth like a fish. She painted them. And then together. She rubbed a lipstick onto my cheeks to make them rosy. Beautiful, she said. She held up a mirror. I looked into it. Well? she said, as she took the mirror away. I asked for it back again. How do you like it?

I nodded.

You are the most beautiful in all the world. Fathers tell their daughters this. And in the evening, once she had left, I washed it off. I filled the sink with water and scrubbed at my face with a flannel and soap. I could still taste the lipstick. In the evening. In the eve. Because it was she who stole the day.

My mother stopped coming as often as she used to. He was glad of that. He was glad that she was no longer there when he sat down for dinner. He hated serviettes and she always put out serviettes. And then she would complain that he stained them. She said once she went to a restaurant where they refused to serve spaghetti bolognaise because the tomato sauce was too difficult to remove from the white cloth. He thought this was stupid and told her so; that serviettes were meant to wipe the mess up. But this was not why she stopped coming, I do not think. I think she did not know what to say to me. What to say to me for a whole day. It was hard, because she came by train and the train took a couple of hours and because of this she thought she should get her money's worth on her ticket and stay the whole day. She did not need to, I tried to tell her this. But she would insist. Often I was glad that she did, even though I knew she would have preferred not to. She had to help me bathe and she did not like my nakedness. It frightened her. I saw her look at me the way I remembered myself looking at girls' breasts when I was getting them myself – staring at their breasts instead of their faces and forgetting that they could see where my eyes were gazing. It was not that I forgot, I did not know. I did not know that you could look at someone's eyes and know what they were seeing.

That was how my mother looked at me. At my stomach. At my thin sack self.

I would climb carefully into the bath and she would wash me. She did not want to at first. I felt her hand hesitate behind me, but she did – touch me eventually. She went back all the way to when I was a baby. She went back all the way to when we would have a bath together and I would lie flat over her stomach and her breasts to keep warm, the thin film of water warm between us, and she would pour water over my back and sing to me.

She did not come to visit me for weeks. She phoned to tell me this, she said she was busy. That was good. I was glad she was busy. It was good to be busy. I remembered this. Then she said she had been praying for me.

Sometimes I hear the sound of the movies when people speak to me. I heard the movies then. I was sitting on the red itchy seats in the dark and listening to what my life sounded like. It went like this: that noise, very close up, of someone hearing a voice through the phone and then the person listening swallows with their mouth slightly open and then breathes in. A sort of wet clicking noise. Like the slow unfolding of an insect.

I did not believe in God. I did not think she did either. I asked her this and she said to me that sometimes it is all you have left. Not me, I said. I hope you don't think that's me because it's not. I have lots left, I said. I have lots.

You're a good girl. You're a good girl, she said.

I remember I banned her from calling me that when I was twelve. Call me anything, I said, except for that.

My mother wanted perfect things. This was how she wanted the man she loved, and it was also how she wanted me: a daughter who would be loving and confiding the way she thought all good daughters should be. But it became increasingly evident that somehow we had both failed her.

The first floor of the hotel I am staying in is above street level and on the eastern side there are small white balconies attached to each room so as to catch the morning sun. Beneath these a path runs alongside the hotel and it is this path that I take in the mornings on my way into the city.

This morning I heard two people talking. They are the same two people that I hear every morning when I go out, providing that I leave at the same time – eight-thirty so that I can be in the office at the Quay by nine. They occupy the third apartment to the left on the ground floor. It is a large room, which is why I think of it as an apartment, for I saw into it one evening through the lace curtains: there was a bar and a living area, there must have been bedrooms off to the sides.

I slowed my pace when I heard the couple – just the sound of them for I could not quite make out what they were saying, although I would have liked to, if only for the strange shapes their voices made, as they do each time I have heard them – but thought it would be conspicuous should I stop. For each morning it is the same: his voice underneath hers. Hers above. As though he were seated at the table and she were serving him, even though they are paying to stay in a hotel.

I recognised this pattern in their voices, the strange ways by which we accommodate each other. We had suffered this before. Servitude and its abuses.

(Red apples I brought you–

No. I wanted green.)

There had been rain in the afternoon, when he climbed into bed beside her, already starting to kiss her when he stopped and held her away from him. Green light came in the room as the rain ended. She looked at him from this arm's distance and said, no, let me, and began to undress him, slowly, under the covers, then came out and kissed him on the mouth on his head and his neck, wrapping herself around him. He lay there, on his back with his face to the ceiling, and let her. He said, do to me, his eyes open at first, then closed. Do to me anything, he said.

My body holds the memory of yours. We are vessels. We have said that muscle holds memory, but it is more than muscle, it is flesh. We use something more than meat to make and lose and choose our memory.

In the daytime Isabel came with flowers and put them in a milk bottle filled with water, their stems stripped of leaves so they could drink. She carried them in, her hands dripping, and said, here, I have brought you these.

I am the receiver of gifts. I am the host of the house. Everyone brings me things. And she leans over me and places them on the windowsill.

As the light reached for them she said, he's not here again. No, he is at work, and she said, he leaves you alone too often, and I said that I'm not totally incapable and that we need some money. We have to live on something, I said. I could look after you, she said. I know that we all want to have something to care for. Better than him, she added, and touched her hand to my head because she was standing beside me.

I turned my face away and looked at the flowers. Honeysuckle and the last roses from our garden. I can see where the petals have been eaten at by insects and the bottom of the stems where they were broken from the plant and their coloured faces are turning to me and she is talking and she says, I have been thinking, have been thinking, about how best we might – and I was wondering, while over the top of her I can hear the flower heads screaming. She did not ask if she could cut them, she did not ask to come into my room and I can hear the pain of them, their long necks sucking at the water looking for what they belonged to because the rest of them is outside, in the garden, wondering where these pieces have gone. The green light of their stems filling up the spaces of what was taken. In here. In here, I say. In a glass bottle with their heads hanging on a cold rim and I said, take them away. I said, you didn't ask me and she thought I meant whether she could enter my room without knocking and she said she always had before and I said, you should always ask before you take something, take something away from itself. Take them away, I can hear them crying, and she says, there is nothing crying and then, did you hear anything I have been saying?

I have been speaking to you, what is wrong with you they are a gift you need something fresh in here and I picked them for you. I looked at her. She looked back at me, then leaned across, lifted the flowers off the windowsill and took them away.

I remember the sound of her voice against the glass, and soon after the door closing behind her downstairs. I cut and wrapped my fear then and put it in a lunch box. Eat it, my mother would say, eat what you are given, but I was always the bad one who threw it away. She squashed the bread when she cut the sandwiches, squashed the tomato. Now it is my turn and I have packed it into my clothes too.

Outside feathers moved so fast they sounded like water and the light came in, slicing through the window and onto the wall behind me. She said orange, that summer air is orange, but this is gold. The whole room, gold as the outside of the bell I am housed in.

There are shadows as the sun moves, forming four dark bars across the window, and I am inside a bell tower, inside shadow, as the bells begin their final ringing. It is the sound of pain far away, the singing that is the swell of metal after it has come against itself. While the chime, my tongue, drums in the darkness of my mouth as the rest of the day happens to itself, and later I find again, find that it has, as it does, that it has come to finishing. (My turn next, the hours say, my turn, and I allow them, like moving for a vehicle in the fast lane.)

His car arrived home. He turned the engine off, opened the door and pulled himself out. I went out to him and said, hello darling, and he kissed me and said, hello darling too. I smiled. He knew why I was smiling and smiled back. I was smiling because I had won, because he had said he would never call me darling, that he would call me honey or sweetheart but not darling. I don't know why he didn't want to call me darling but he didn't and now he had and he knew this and he knew that I knew and that I had won. Alright he said, alright, and took my hand and we went inside and he poured himself a drink and we sat down together in the evening.

I dream again now and I continue to dream of him. None of it is make-believe. It is as though we had died and were given our chance all over again. The water – the lake – the park and the footpath with the city behind it. There is the concrete bright in the sunlight and white boats. It is lunchtime. There are people everywhere, running, walking, lying in the sun. At the side of the path is a man selling ice-creams, strawberry and chocolate, all the other flavours having run out, which is a shame for he wanted vanilla, vanilla and hazelnut were your favourites, but it is too hot even for ice-cream and we only want something to drink.

We walk together and I hold my arms up to shade my face. Music comes from the boats tied up to the wharf, while people lie in the cool dark of the cabins. No one is sailing. The air is still. The boats click together in the water. They will be moved soon. It will be cold again, colder than we have known it, and the whole harbour will freeze over. Aside from this it is all just as it was before, except that up ahead at the end of the pier is a ferris wheel. Its thin white frame is faint in the distance. We could see its red carriages turning slowly as though it were above the water and not the land. I have no recollection of us speaking but we must have agreed to get on it for the next thing was that we bought an ice-cream each because we could not find a drink, and ate them while waiting in line for the ride. Although we do not get on, we never get on. We watch the red carriages come around and around while we eat our ice-creams and the carriages keep coming around and they come around and the more they come around the more they look like cages and not carriages at all and the more they come around the less we see anyone ever get out of them and we do not know anyone who gets in, although people must, we knew that, everyone was there paying their money and we had paid but we never got on.

He became changed too. He stopped coming to see me in the mornings. In the evenings he increasingly did not want to eat. He continued to wash me though, helping me in and out of the bath, and would bring me food when I needed it. He still did all of those things. But it became different. He did not know any more what to talk to me about, as though I had been gone for so long that there was no longer anything to say. I had nothing to speak of. And at night he no longer tried to touch me. Good night, he would say and fall asleep.

I do not know what happened to him then. He did not say. I have drawn many conclusions since but I do not know if they are the truth. I had been sick for so long and we were both so tired of it.

He still brought me anything I wanted. He would ask me, he would say, is there anything I can get you, is there anything I can do? And I would say, no, there is nothing that I want. There is nothing that you can do other than what you are doing already, and he would leave.

It makes sense then that he should have begun to turn away and find, where he could, other things to fill his life with. I would have let go of him then if I could. I knew he was not happy. If I could only have given him some ease. My own ease. For I had stopped fighting then. If illness was what I had been given then I accepted that. It was he who hadn't. As for happiness, what was there to be said? We had had happiness. We had been to the beach, eaten chocolate, danced. We had had more happiness than we thought possible. But it was an excited happiness, it had been huge and it was not what I wanted any more. I was too tired for that. I only wanted peace.

I should have told him to leave, I should have said to him that he should not stay and that he did not need to keep caring for me like he did. He needed more than what we had and I could not give it to him. But I did not say that. I did not grant him this even when he said to me, send me away, please, send me away. How could I have been the one to ask him to leave.

It was something old and something new. It was something borrowed and something – Blue is the colour of, and green is for – And red? Red is always sex. And blood and death.

And he needed me. Didn't you. You needed something. But what was it, Love?, I don't know. We always need more than we think, and then when we take all that we have thought of taking we only end up throwing it all away again, throwing the baby out with the bath water, and then there we are – back where we started from. What was it, Love? (Love, cross it out, no, write love again) love? I was red once.

And now, in the middle of the night, it comes over me and over and over me again and I am awake and when I wake I find him all through me and I can smell the ocean. I can taste it in my throat and then

I see it – coming slowly at us through the window, it's blue-grey body ebbing and breathing through the open glass, across the wall with the white and green wallpaper and down onto the floor and towards me, the water is coming for me, the water is coming for us again – the way blue fills a body until it ceases to speak.

A tap runs. Morning. There are the muted movements of bodies above and beneath me. To the sides. How do you want to be buried. I told you to burn me. Listen.

A man calls out to another man in the street below.

Wanting. Always wanting.

One morning he said that he no longer knew if he was dead or alive. What is the difference between dying and ceasing to live. How he could continue managing to manage, but nothing more.

He was walking down the stairs, leaning against the wall instead of the railing, and then stopped. He sat down, shaking, the back of him – I could see his humped form trembling as he started to cry.

I was the one who held him.

He said he didn't know why. Said he couldn't help it. It's okay. It's okay, I said. I held him. Or I tried. He didn't move his body towards me easily and I had to tug and pull at him to get him into my arms. Finally he was there.

The crying was an accident. It was not the real thing. He didn't mean it, he said. He was something different from sad. He said he thought he was losing his mind.

Bullshit, I said. What do you mean? You look fine to me. No, he said.

Outside I could hear the rain coming towards us. Hitting the trees, then the trees closer and finally it was on top of us. Eventually he got up. He pulled himself up with the wall and went to the bedroom for his shoes. He sat at the end of the bed and tried to undo the laces. They were in a knot. I tried to undo them too. I couldn't. You shouldn't take them off so fast, I said, and he threw the shoe at the cupboard but it missed. He put his old shoes on. The black ones with the frayed laces.

It has been more than a week now and he has not come. We are playing a game now. We have played it once before. It began late one night, while we were waiting for a train in the subway. We were going to dinner at a friend's place and I cannot recall what it was that began the game but I remember him making a phone call behind me while I waited for the train. I had given him some change and he went around the other side of the platform to use the pay phone. The game began as an argument but we pretended it was a game because we did not want to argue. It was about the phone call, I remember. He phoned his children to say good night to them; he did not always do this but he wanted to that night and he spoke to their mother.

Did she ask where you were? I asked when he returned.

No.

Did you tell her?

No.

I wanted him to tell her. I wanted her to know that he could not talk because he was in company, because he was on his way out to have dinner with friends who she did not know. It was not as though I was tired of deceit, there had never been deceit. It was all long over, but I was tired of diplomacy, I was tired of that politeness that serves only to avoid the truth. I was angry that he had not said anything. I said nothing but he knew this. I turned away from him but he had already opened the paper and was reading. I hated this. I walked away, closer to the end of the platform. I could be unreasonable. He knew this. I told him that I could not stand him talking about his children but he couldn't understand this.

The train was late, we were going to be late. He came up behind me then and said, don't smile and so of course I tried not to and of course I did. He saw this and he said so. Don't smile, he said, and don't look at me. You are not to look at me or speak to me until I say so.

The train still did not come and the people around us looked sideways at us as though we were arguing. It was easier for him, he had the paper and leaned against the wall behind me, while I had nothing to read and could only look at the billboards or the ground. And he tried to provoke me, coming closer, asking me a question, walking close enough so that I could look sideways at him, and then when the train finally came I was afraid he would not get on and so I had to look about to find him, not knowing if he was watching me or not. He saw me look and said, don't look. I'm not, I said.

We got on the train. It was very crowded and we had to sit in two seats facing one another. I watched the ground. Every now and then I could tell that he was watching me and then was not. Once or twice I almost laughed and he saw this. It was good then to remember that it was a game and that I was not really furious with him, but it was a game and I would not lose.

The train came to our stop. I stood up and passed him without a glance. He followed me. We crossed the road to the bus stop and waited for the one we needed. I stood away from him and many buses came but none of them was ours. This one, I called out when the right one arrived and he ran ahead of me, but it was full before we could get on and he turned to me, I had been watching his back, and when he turned I met his eyes. Don't look at me, he said. I did not, I replied.

But you spoke, he said.

I had to.

I was angry. He was cheating. I had not lost. Another bus came. We got on. I sat down next to another man and he took a seat further up behind me. I knew he did not know where to get off but I was not going to tell him. He would have to watch me. At our stop I got off quickly, but when I looked behind me he was not there, I saw him sitting still at the back of the bus reading the paper.

I called out. He looked up and jumped off the bus. We were looking at each other then and I had spoken. I started walking and he followed me. Should we buy some wine? he asked. I did not reply at first then asked if the game was over.

I did not know we were still playing, he said.

You never ended it, I told him.

It is over then. In fact, he said, I almost went home because I did not know why you were not speaking to me.

You said not to.

I didn't think you would take it so seriously.

And now it is as though we play this game again.

My mother came when she could. Not as often as she had promised but often enough. When she arrived the dog would greet her with a wagging tail even though it was nearly blind and could not recognise her. It must have gone by smell, that strange similar smell that we have, my mother and I, being of the same family.

When I went out to greet her she told me that I didn't have to. Sit down, she said, and busied herself while I rested, watching her cook dinner although it was hardly past the time of breakfast. She put the kettle on and, while she waited for it to boil, came up behind me as I sat with my face resting against the table and stroked my head. I had seen her stroke her own head like this when I was a child. When she would lay her face on the kitchen table in the river house and stroke her own hair from behind, touching herself with the memory of her own mother's hands. This was the same touch, and as she touched she murmured things, how everything passes, how lovely the day was, that just yesterday she was thinking. It was hot and the table was cold on my face.

She says, come on, let's go down to the water. She took me. We walked along the edge of the road with me on the inside, so if a car came, she said, it would hit her first. When we get there she undresses in the open and leaves her clothes in a pile on the grass. She wades in and swims. It is lovely, she calls out, it is lovely.

By the water is an old man with his grandson. The man has a toy boat tied to a length of string and as he pulls it along the water's edge the boy chases it.

The boat is always out of reach and the boy runs with his hands out. His grandmother stands further back on the grass in a white skirt that rustles in the breeze and laughs at the two of them.

Come on, mother calls, come on, trying to coax me into the water. I can't, I say. Come on, she says, softly, softly, her arms opening to me. I am already in past my knees and she takes hold of my waist and the water rises against it, bit by bit, until we are floating in the deep. Then she brings me back a little, her arms resting along the water's edge, the rest of her body lifted in the water, lifting my body, her daughter. The curve of my back against her belly, my neck limp against her shoulder. Just her voice in my ear and water.

I do not know in what way flesh leaves itself. And as the body goes, what goes with it. The question remains of how much of me, over time, has departed. For they say there are memories in our muscles and in our bones.

I thought sometimes that I was beginning to know something of how the earth was formed. Sitting still with itself, prepared for nothing to happen, prepared for nothing. And then there is a becoming, of caves and roots, depths and fluid, where only a moment ago, or perhaps it was a million years, there were flat dry plains.

In the evening he tapped at the bathroom door with the back of his knuckles. Behind it he heard her move

148

in the water. Do you want me to wash your back? he asked.

If you like.

He opened the door and found her already drawn in against her knees, just her back showing, curled up with the sides of her breasts pressing against her thighs. He moved to the stool behind her and lathered soap between his palms. He moved his hands down her back. She flinched. He tried not to notice, rubbing her back all over, and her neck, behind her ears, before washing the soap off with cups of water.

Do you want me to help you out? he asked, holding the towel open for her to step into. I can manage, she said and he put the towel back on the rack.

He left quietly but she heard him wait outside the door, listening to the unfolding of her body from the water and for the squeak of the stool legs as she rested a moment before dressing.

He described me once as familiar. It was a word I had always associated with things that were worn and dusty. And yet when he said it there was a newness to it, as though my familiarity was original. It is well known that partners eventually become like teacups to one another but this did not seem to bother him. Quite the opposite, in fact. It was with excitement that he realised he could love something so known, and because he continued to love it, and because he realised that he loved it still, it became brand new again.

He had a word for this. He called it fondness. But try as we might, eventually we changed. And we became strange, with him saying that it was our strangeness that had become everything. That was what he feared then. That was what we both grew to fear – that we had come to each other by accident and it had become impossible to leave.

At night then he touched me as if I were some strange animal, the way one reaches out to stroke an unfamiliar horse – with love, with every effort to mask fear. His hand reaching up to my face so that I could see it coming, so that I would not draw away from him, startled and unsettled. I flinched as his hand reached my cheek but he did not move away, instead he cupped his palm around the side of me and, like a good animal, sensing the comfort of flesh, I let him leave it there.

But he did not stay. Late that night I heard him. He was in bed. He got out. He dressed, left by the front door and drove away.

He went to the city. He told me.

He drove the car, parked and got out. Although it was late the streets were busy and filled with people, with the smell of garbage and beer. Restaurants flashed blue and pink neon from their windows, and at the corner stood a building with a sign that flickered H TEL, a gloved porter standing at its glass door. A man and a woman brushed past him. Excuse me, the woman said, bumping into him on her way out. She was facing her date as they walked, and he had said something, causing her to erupt in laughter and throw her whole head towards the sky, forgetting to watch where she was going.

Up ahead there was music. A man came out of a pub and walked onto the road. Another passed by with a dog, and there were people dressed up, strutting as couples and in crowds, while on the next corner a man yelled passages from the Bible into a foam cup as though it were a microphone. His hands shook as he rolled a cigarette.

You're smoking, she had said to him one night when they spoke on the phone.

Yes.

I can hear it, she said. Exhale. I like the sound of it. She said she could hear the sound of the street – traffic, and a couple fighting. He described them: the woman walking quickly ahead of the man who chased after her and called out. She turned to him and yelled back. She was wearing a dress, carried a handbag. It was small bag, he said, made of black leather. It was slipping off her shoulder because she was trying to walk so fast, which was difficult for her dress was tight around her legs and meant she could not stride.

Across the road was a bar. A dim light came from the back of it and there were people pressed against the glass of the front window. He went in, ordered a drink and turned to see the woman who had bumped into him in the street sitting beside him, drinking beer with the same man who had made her laugh and who now moved his hand up and down her spine as they spoke. She had a strong body, tall, and as she leaned her elbow on the bar he could make out the smooth muscle of her arm.

He ordered another drink and watched the woman next to him, her spine, the groove on either side of the bone. The man was pressing his fingers into it and touching her hair, the stray pieces that had escaped around her face, his eyes moving quickly across it as though he were looking for something.

He turned away and watched the glass in his hands and the cigarette, his fingers trembling, as though something of him were knocked away by each thing he touched. He drank quickly then left. Crumpled, she had said once, she felt crumpled. There was smoke in his face and the smell of sweat as he headed for the door. And he thought of her, how she used stay with him in the city in the beginning and never remember spare clothes. One night he said he'd wash for her what she had. She left him a small pile on the bed and before he cleaned them he held them to his face.

She had said then, you are mistaken. You are confusing love with the absence of pain.

But he said, no. Nothing like you has ever happened to me before.

He knew where to go.

There were three doors to pass through before he entered: a metal grate, followed by a wooden door then a glass one. Both the metal grate and the wooden door were open. The glass one was closed and behind it a woman in a short black dress and strappy shoes stood talking into a mobile phone. She saw him approach and opened the door, still talking. He had drunk more than he thought and he leaned against the wall as he waited.

The woman told him she'd be with him in a minute. Her voice was strained by a grossly malformed jaw, out of proportion to the other features of her face. He looked away and shoved his hands into his pockets. The woman finished the phone call. She said hello although she didn't smile. Yes? she said.

He said he'd like, he'd like–

I'll take you through, she said. Have you been here before?

No.

Would you like to see the girls first, or shall I show you around?

The girls, he said.

She took him through to a living room where five women were sitting on red velveteen lounges. The walls were red, everything was red, even the ceilings. In the corners of the room were potted plants and a piano, photographs on the walls, black and white pictures of women's faces and city streets. A TV was on, one girl flicked impatiently through the channels, another scanned a magazine.

The woman with the jaw asked if there were any he liked. He didn't care, but understood he was required to choose. He pointed to a woman sitting on the lounge filing her nails. Lisa, the woman said. She looked up. Said hello. She had doe eyes, underlined so heavily they drooped, and stiff dark hair. Come with me, she said. He followed her up the stairs, the TV shifting channels behind him.

She took him into a room. Simple, not plush like the living room, and closed the door. He could smell alcohol on her skin and cheap perfume. He leaned forward for her face. She put her hand up against his head and held it while he groped. It was dark. He was drunk. He undressed her roughly, taking off her clothes and pushing them aside where he could, then he was pushing her down, or falling, and she didn't resist. His stomach touched her skin and he kissed her face, the taste of make-up, her hands touching his cheek to keep their mouths apart, holding him there, holding his face and moving on top of him. He wanted the floor, he wanted something hard, and he found himself fucking her, fucking when he knew he didn't want to, and then sobbing because he was feeling her while he was feeling nothing, pushed against the floor with pieces of her body in his mouth and telling her then to make some sound, to sing, he said, sing! Then that he was coming, that he was going to come he was going to come, he said and doing everything he could not to and not to cry out, the way you scream at something to send it away and scream because you want it back and scream because you know that none of it is what you want anyway and none of it is enough or it is too much.

(This is the after life, he thought. When all your organs and treasures have been stolen and put on display in sterile glass cabinets in another country. It is not hot there. It is air conditioned for customer comfort. And this one here, they say, pointing, this one here was for luck. And he could understand why a mad man would cut his ears off. If you were insane, naturally you would think you were hearing things because you had ears. And bear the soul's suffering on the body. It is the fashionable thing now, he thought, to console madness with the guise of genius or grief. But it is only human. Madness. And it is genius that does not exist.)

He pulled himself out of her and rolled off. She got up. The dark of her back was towards him. She said she needed to turn on the light. It blinded him. He put his arm across his face and could smell her all over it. His pants were still at his ankles. She said something to him, but he didn't hear her. She was facing the wall. She turned, looked at him just once. He found his clothes and left.

He returned home late the next night, unshaven and wearing the same clothes, a shirt, long pants, his blue jacket. He eased the car carefully into the drive, hoping, I imagine, that I was asleep.

I was not. I was making something to eat. He came in and leaned against the bench on the other side of the kitchen. He watched me. He had been drinking. He must have been drinking as he drove home. I was slicing a carrot with a blunt knife which slipped and cut my thumb. It began to bleed. I dropped the knife, put my thumb to my mouth. He came up behind me, took my thumb and put it in his own mouth. He put his hand on my back and I turned to him, our faces were not far apart, his eyes moved across me. He looked frightened. What? I said. He didn't reply. He continued to look at me. What is it? Come outside, he said, and he told me.

Tell me, he said one night, why it is that you love me, what it is in particular.

I gave him a list. He did not like it. It was not that it was bad, but it was not so different from the reasons that others had given before. A list that goes something like: kindness, love, humour, followed by talents – cooking, talking, singing. Then more general things, although no less important, such as intelligence, hair, eyes, teeth etc.

But he knew these things already. Or if they were traits he did not wish to accept, then he was familiar with his own arguments against them. Kindness, for example. That kind of warmth that cannot help but present itself to the front of things.

(Red apples. No, I wanted green.)

He wanted the source of love that overrode all our particular and fallible arguments, and naturally I could not give him this. That is, there was no word for such a thing that would not destroy the very body it was designed to accommodate. But he thought that through such a thing he would be able to see himself differently. He wanted to think that I recognised something in him that no one else had seen, and could thereby show him this self that he hoped he could be. How was it, he thought, that I myself could be some kind of original and yet love him for the same things? I think he thought that because of us he would be like a new person. Better even.

I said it did not matter. I made myself look him in the eye and say this – but I knew that it did, and I knew when he looked back at my eyes that he could tell I was not all there behind them.

He said he didn't know how it happened. He said he was drunk, they were both drunk. I shuddered at this, at the thought of him desperate and full of grief. And sobbing – how he sobs after too much wine, turning always first to sadness rather than anger. But it was pointless for me to match his sorrow with fury.

Maybe, he said, it was some sort of goodbye. But we both knew that she was not the thing that needed leaving.

We stared at the night. I was silent. I did not behave badly. I was not angry, although he expected that I would be. He lit up a cigarette; this habit of his that he called a vice did not bother me, although I felt that it should. In fact I had come to like the way it caused him, out of kindness, to turn his face from me.

I also looked away.

Speak to me, he said, turning back to me. I did not know what to say. However much I would have liked a case to argue I did not feel I had one. Possibly I was in a position to make demands, to rail about betrayal. But there was every reason for me not to. The fact that time had passed between us was my only defence. But I could not say that I had been there for all of it. I knew that my body was weak, not out of any fault of my own, but still, I knew that every time he approached me I turned away. He knew I did not want his tongue in my mouth. And it was not even that we did not or could not speak, we could, in the past we always had, and we spoke to each other well. But after years of illness there was nothing much left to say.

I wish now that I had not been so forgiving. For it was not as though any of it came without pain. It crippled me to think of his grief and it disgusted me to think of his desire, imagining him fucking and sobbing and fucking, the two of them, and I thought of the woman, I imagined that she would have known he was only with her because he had failed to be with another. But maybe it was not like that, maybe it was not like that at all. I thought only that it was better that it was with a stranger – that way it was only about their bodies, and had nothing to do with old love or with the past.

Why? I said. He began to explain but I said, stop.

(I remember how badly he was burnt one summer. How at night his body continued to hold the heat of the sun inside it. Burn, he said once. You make me burn. Taking the heat and the heat of a person until it hurts.)

It was the heartskin losing its definition.

I did not want to know who the woman was. I did not want to know if she was ugly or beautiful. Both possibilities would have been bad. I had thought, when previously considering his betrayal in theory, that I would have wanted to know, but no, I did not. I might if he were to tell me that he thought he loved her.

He would say thought, he would say he thought he loved her in the hope that he might be convinced that he did not. If he only thought he loved her, but it could be proved to him that he didn't, he would not have to make any decision. He could just fuck her. But he didn't love her. He did just fuck her. But he did it with something, with sorrow, with a sorrow that can be as intimate as any joy, that can be, like love, both a great burden and a great relief.

If he were to love someone else I would want to know about her in order to know what she was that I was not. But I know what I am not. And I knew what I was not then. I am very aware of what we did not have. We did not touch or talk the way we once did, we forgot to kiss. Yet we cared. On the contrary, it was the fact that we cared so much – he cared so much, too much – that caused us in the end to become too fragile, so that there was no longer anything that was not deliberate or habitual between us.

It was not hurt. It was something else. Outside of me. Him, outside of me. It was the thought that he had desires that I did not know of, that desire was not a finite thing. That somehow there would always be more and it would always be different. And I could not try to chase it to completion all the time, I knew that neither of us would always be what we wanted and because of this I would never know him completely.

160

So I was sad. I was terribly sad. He was asking me again to talk to him, but I did not, I could not, I did not know what to say.

Why do people come together? I asked him late that night while he pretended he was asleep. I knew he was pretending, I could feel it. He did not answer, and I imagine that it was because on that night it felt as though people came together only to help each other be apart. Then I said, rolling over, that tonight it felt like there were too many bones growing in my head, and that he was one of them.

I untangled myself and got up, pulled on a jumper and went to the window. My breath fogged the cold glass. I took a spare blanket and told him I didn't think I could stay in the same room as him and went downstairs to the couch.

He would have liked her to be angry, or more violently sad, to have had some sort of response that in turn might have evoked some feeling in him. He had imagined the scenario – that she would hold him by the throat in the dark once she knew what had happened, that she would be on top of him with her thumbs at his neck, and he would look up at her, all dark in the room, and he would say, kill me. He would say, sometimes I think I am already dead.

After she had said to him that she did not want to know, he wanted to tell her everything, down to the finest detail. Tell her about the woman, Lisa – her body, her legs, the scent of her skin. And he would use her name, Lisa, as though they were intimate. Instead, as she left the room, he said – half to himself, half to the empty space she was leaving him in – I no longer recognise myself, and then that he was sorry, that he was so sorry, and began to cry. Oh God, she said, please, don't do this, and left the room anyway.

In the morning I sat at Isabel's table, cross-legged on the chair, while she leaned against the sink, eating the last of the porridge from the saucepan. At her feet the dog sniffed about for fallen food.

I would have liked to cry when I told her but I didn't. Instead I watched my hands. From some distance I heard myself talk and I told her what he had done. As though it were nothing, because I knew that it was – nothing. Those details, those details that I would have preferred to remove and that I said were not the things that counted.

But I did not want to offer her his excuses, I knew she would not take them.

Where is he now? she asked, as though he were a criminal we were to trace. She always thought of him, I think, as some kind of criminal, keeping me while never having done enough to earn me.

Inside. In the kitchen.

She told me that I could not stay. I could not let it go on like this.

I tried to tell her that it was not like that.

Isabel turned, filled the saucepan with water and leaned across the sink towards the window. Her voice bounced off the glass, tell me then, how it is, she said, sitting down.

It's too big, too big to begin.

She shifted in her seat. Her hands searching out the edges of the cup and holding onto it. She told me what it was that I deserved. Essentially this amounted to more than him, and I wondered how she knew, when she had not seen how little I had been prepared to give. He cooked for me and I did not eat it. If he tried to kiss me I hardly opened my mouth. When he came home in the evenings I no longer made any effort to speak. And I could not tell any longer how much of this was due to sickness and how much was not. I did not expect her to understand this. Even though she had seen me sick and had washed me and cared for me. And for her I had always been careful to be kind, with her I had not been difficult.

We each looked away. She was not saying what she wanted from me. Yet she seemed to think that he was stealing something that was hers, or taking for himself what should only be mine. How could he state any claim to my body and then take another's? But she did not say this. And she did not know how much of myself I had not given to him.

In the dark kitchen with the day behind her I saw a parrot fly in and out of a tree half hidden by the shape of her head. The red and green bird flashed, it seemed, in and out of her hair as she picked at the rim of the teacup where it had chipped, while I had a vague memory of my father telling me how we think in shapes and how we can share these – a blue triangle and a yellow square, the white oval of her face that she gave to me.

But she did not say what it was that she was thinking. Her cheeks flushed and she concentrated on looking into her cup. The rim chinking and chinking as her nails picked at the broken bit. I really must fix my hands, she said, taking them away from the cup and inspecting them. And at the back of my throat I could taste something. It was thick and dark, like the bush after it is burnt. Like ash and black earth. It tasted solid. As though I had swallowed her and was bringing her back up.

I do not understand women. And even though I am one of them I have never understood what one is supposed to do with them.

A fortune-teller once told me that I had been a man in my previous life and that I had not resolved this. She said that if I paid her one hundred dollars US she could remove my maleness for me.

I did not do this though, and so after I had faced Isabel I went home.

All day he and I did not speak. At night he asked if I wanted to go for a drive. Yes, alright, I said. He had not asked me this in years. Good, he said, get dressed.

It was late, we drove to the highway and took a right turn. Few other cars were on the road. He put both hands on the wheel and kept them there. He did not look at me. I put my hand on his leg. I took it away again. There were the green lights on the dashboard. Green time.

Where are we going?

Nowhere.

I like going nowhere. We had not gone nowhere together in years.

We drove in silence. I watched the car lights on the other side of the road come at me.

Talk to me, he said.

What do you want me to say? I asked. It was a reasonable question. It still is. He could not answer it. Eventually he said, I'm not all here, am I? And I said, no. Neither of us were. He pulled over. I don't know how it was that we had disappeared.

Tell me what it is. But I turned away from him and could only think of why it is that we make ourselves so difficult to love, why it is that when we are asked to speak we refuse.

This is not healthy, he said. No, I agreed, and I wanted to laugh – as if two people together could ever be hygienic and I thought of us, clean, like fridges.

He was still holding onto the steering wheel. It was cold inside the car. We turned around.

I'm leaving, I said. And he said, yes.

I went into the bookshop today where we used often to meet. It was early evening and although I knew he would not be there I hoped somehow that he would. He used to work around the corner and would meet me here when he had finished, with me arriving purposely early so he would have to find me. We would agree to meet during the day and I would say, so you will come and find me then? And he would say, yes, please. Let me come and find you. And when he saw me he would say my name and sometimes I would hear it and pretend I had not, pretending I was engrossed in a book so he would have to come closer and say my name again.

I walked in, slowly, around the way he would have once come, and looked for him. Of course he was not there, but I walked on, towards the corner where we would meet. I did not want to go there, everything in my body refused, I had not seen such an empty space of books in all my life, never had they seemed so pointless, so un-worth reading. But I had to go there. I had to progress from where I was standing and look to the shelf. I had not gone there entirely without reason. There was a book I needed to find and I had been everywhere else in the city before I had decided to go there. I had not wanted to go. It was the last place left. And yet I didn't have to go. I could have phoned to see if they had the book, I could have paid for it over the phone and picked it up at the counter in order to avoid walking the way he had walked. But I did not. I decided I would go and look for it myself. If he were here now he would tell me that I should ask for help, that maybe it was shelved elsewhere, but I would not ask, I never do. I have never learnt how to ask for this.

I was facing the books then and already I could see him – walking towards me, half seeing him from the corner of my eye and pretending I had not, waiting, as I said, for him to approach me, to say my name, for him to watch me just a moment before saying anything, and then later he would say, and you had your hair down, and you had your coat on, telling me how he saw me for that moment before I knew he was there. And he would have said my name so that others would hear it, and I would look up and he would ask what I was reading and I would show him a million things and I would watch his hands turn the pages and he would read and I would point to paragraphs and we would look at the pages together. I would be leaning against his shoulder then and I would smell him, the smell of mints and cigarettes, alcohol if he was late and the rain, and the rain, bright drops pearled over the shoulders of his black suit. So often it rained. And then we would go home, he would say, come on, and I would say, yes, let's go.

But he was not there. He would never be there again and I knew this. I stood before the books. I could not read the titles. I knew already that they would not have the one that I wanted. I knew this before I came. I could have phoned but I did not. I wanted to go there. I wanted to go there because it was where we had always been. I looked. There were still titles that had been there when we were together and there were new ones. But not the one that I wanted.

I made myself leave. I made myself turn, walk away and leave.

Our past is redundant now. It has no possibility for the future. I am in its uselessness and I have come to the end of it. I have taken our history as far as I can and we have run out. We have fallen short of everything else we could have been. We end here and I do not know what begins.

You belong here now. You are everywhere you are not. I look for you everywhere. For a man in a suit in the street.

What have I done, you would ask, with the years between us? I have worked, I would say. I have worked hard like I once used to and dealt coldly with the world. Time passes and I have thought of you little, I would say. I have tried to keep you there, in that distance, have tried to make sensible decisions about irrational things – that you were not right, that I was not right, that it would have always been impossible for a million reasons. My mother told me all of these things. And then I saw you. And now I see you everywhere. And I have forgotten everything. Who would have thought that you, who believed in so little, who had no faith, would be the one to teach some strange sort of belief to me. You, who are happening to me now in your absence far more than you ever did when you were here. You are, as I said, everywhere you are not. I look for you on every street corner; this morning I thought I saw you on a bus, I thought I recognised the back of your head, your hair, you were sitting down, reading the paper; ridiculous, I knew it was ridiculous, it was raining, I could not see, and aside from this I know you would not catch a bus to work, I know you do not ever come that way. It was only a man in a suit. There are so many men in suits here.

I walked out of the bookshop. I remember. I remember making myself walk out of the bookshop and walk away. I saw myself hold out my hand to flag down a bus. I paid for my ticket. I do not recall where I asked to go. I sat down.

A man behind me was on his way home. He took out his phone from a brown leather briefcase and pressed in a number. He got the answering machine and left a message. He said, hello darling, I'm on my way home. I made the eight-fifteen bus. If you could call me when you get this. A few minutes later his phone rang. It was his hello darling. They spoke about the day. He asked if she'd had a good walk, if they had gone yet. Is there dinner made? he asked. She must have said yes, his darling. There must have been others eating because he said, if there are any leftovers it would be nice to have some. The line was breaking up. She couldn't hear him. He said, if there are any leftovers it would be nice to have some. He said it louder: I said, if there are any leftovers it would be nice to have some.

It is a longing now that has grown wild. This is not love. What is the difference? I asked my mother this. She said, longing is an ideal. Love is comfortable. It is not love if it leaves you lonely.

You can only long for something that you do not have and it need not be a whole person. It can be part of them. You can long for part of them even when the rest of them is there. But love loves even what it has not got. It lets you leave things empty and so makes them full.

I am leaving the day after tomorrow and he has not come. In the morning I go down to breakfast in the dining room of the hotel. It is a large room, more of a hall than a room, with a round central dining area and a balcony around that. And it is white, all of it, and all the waiters are dressed in white.

Just for one?

Yes.

I ask for a balcony seat. Just follow me, the waiter says. He has black shoes against the white and they make a light tapping noise as he walks. He offers me a table, pulls the seat out for me and, removing the serviette from the table, shakes it and lays it across my lap. Thank you, I say.

It is early for a weekend breakfast and only two couples are here before me. They are older couples; I have come to notice that it is only the single and the elderly who eat early.

In the centre of the room is a long table which holds an assortment of breakfast foods in silver and china bowls and there are potted palm trees at either end and also at the entrance. On the menu the dining room is called Palm Court and in the evenings I have heard jazz being played on the piano.

From where I sit I can see through the glass doors of the dining room to the glass doors at the entrance of the hotel. I am not watching for him but were he to arrive I would see him before he even reached the front desk to ask for me. But it is not yet nine and although the porter stands there on duty there is no sign of anyone either entering or leaving the building.

A waiter brings coffee. I thank him and sip it while I decide what to eat. The single man who arrived not long after me is already eating – cereal, coffee, toast. He eats quickly, not looking about, and then leaves.

There is no music in here and it is a large space to have no sound. Although they have tried to create some atmosphere with the white, the balconies, palm trees and foreign waiters, it is undercut by the constant clatter of cutlery and heeled footsteps.

More people arrive now, a number of women in company treating themselves, I imagine, to a weekend in town. They are wearing floral dresses. A young woman enters in high-heeled shoes that echo as she walks. She is very tall with long hair, her shirt tied in a knot to show her stomach as she walks around the table one way then the other, picks up a plate, puts it down again and walks towards a second table that holds the drinks. She pours herself a juice and walks back to the centre table. She does all of this very slowly, serving herself some breakfast before walking around the table again and up the stairs to the balcony where she sits down with a man much older than herself. He is not handsome, nor does he talk to her. He eats his croissant with one hand and holds the paper open with the other.

I am no longer as hungry as I thought and ask the waiter if I could just have some toast. I eat a little, drink another coffee. He will not come this morning. I will not call him. I have made a decision that I will not call, that I must not begin any correspondence, that I must, eventually, end even this thinking. And it is this, out of everything, that most pains me: he knows where I am and I know that he will not come. For what would we say. I do not know how we would speak. We have not spoken for so long without sorrow or desire, we have never been neutral as friends are. And I do not know if I want to try. For I do not know which is the sadder of the two: to learn to speak differently, or to not speak at all.

I often used to say to him that I did not do things well in half measures, that when I did something I did it all the way until the very end. I said that was how it would be with the two of us, that I would stay with it until it was dead. It was not like that though. Leaving did not happen in the way I expected. What we left will never be dead. We had to kill it off. We had to bury us alive. That is to say, we could not live in a state of anticipation forever, hoping that I would be well, hoping that when I was well I would not again fall ill, living always for something that had not yet come. It ended because we could not bear it any more. We could not bear the hardest parts of each other without any other fruitfulness. It did not complete itself and we could not complete it and so it remains now as a possibility, as something that was lost.

But we had done with sympathy. I did not want it and he could no longer find it.

This is how the end came.

The night after I told him I was leaving we went out to eat. We were going to have a civilised goodbye. We had spoken of this before, years ago, about how sad it was and how strange that so rarely did one ever end relationships kindly. We tried to do this. We tried to leave with some peace.

The waiter approached our table and opened our wine, holding a white cloth to the bottom of the bottle. He poured us each a full glass and we held them up to each other in a toast. To what? I asked. To your future, he said, to your work, health.

No, I said. To something else.

He looked at me.

To fondness.

That is beautiful, he said, for what else is there to do with something that is being lost other than to lose it. But maybe fondness was not the word with which to toast each other. For I think of it now as a tenderness independent of greater feelings, while perhaps there was something more ferocious between us then, and fondness was not possible. Instead, I led us to believe that we could place ourselves in the past despite our present state of feeling, the way we name a thing not out of truth, but out of a desire for it to exist somehow differently.

I asked him how he thought he might remember this: the years that had passed between us. He said he did not know, that it was not memory yet. But it will be, I said, and you can imagine what it might be like. He was silent. I watched him. Eventually he looked up at me and said that he would always remember it, and that he suspected he would always miss me. I tried not to cry. I looked away, then looked at him again while he looked away.

He was dressed in black. Black jumper. Black pants. The waiter had taken his jacket and hung it by the door. He had not combed his hair. I remember this.

I said I could not bear the thought of him ever loving someone else. He said nothing to this and I did not ask what he was thinking. I knew what he was thinking, he was thinking about the woman before me who must have once said something like this and who had watched him cease loving her and start to love another. There were tears in his eyes. Then he said my name. He said it once then said it again, saying the whole of it, as he always did, and I knew that I would never hear my name said in the same way again, that I could not imagine anyone else saying my name as he did, and I said this.

This is the strangest thing I've ever done, he said. I agreed. I said that I thought it was also the saddest. We could scarcely glance at each other as we said these things, while in between speaking we held each other's eyes for so long that the waiter moved terribly carefully towards us and smiled graciously. We thanked him for everything he did, too often probably, and as he walked away I said that he seemed to think we were in love. I remarked on this as though it were odd, a funny thing that the waiter should think that. Strange, in turn, that I should have said what I did, for even though we were leaving one another I do not think I had ever, have ever, loved anyone more.

I reminded him that he had said once that he would marry me. No, I didn't, he said. I have told you, he said, that I would never marry again.

No, I said, you once said that were I to ask you if you would marry me, you would probably accept. And

I had said the same, although, in the end, neither of us asked.

He remembered this. He took my hand then and looked at me and told me quite seriously that one should never, ever, say such things to anyone, especially in the beginning of love, no matter how much one might feel it. I disagreed. I disagreed. Have you ever said that to anyone else? he asked, presuming that I had. No, I lied. Anything like it? No. Then you said my name again and again and I saw you about to cry.

I had never thought it possible to leave someone with such gentleness and such pain. It was, I am sure, the saddest thing I have ever done. And at the same time, it was also the kindest. Never have I known a greater kindness between two people. Leaving because they loved each other, not because they didn't. It was pure madness. It was the cleanest and most perfect pain.

What were we doing? We were leave-taking. We were taking leave of one another's company. We were both taking and leaving at the same time. And we could not take without that taking leaving something, nor leave without taking.

There are things you know about your own future and I knew this about mine. I knew all along that we would come to this.

I asked him what he was thinking. Just about what you said, he replied. There was a long silence. I watched his face, slack with grief, while he twisted his wine glass round and round on the white tablecloth. What though? I asked and he said, useless things, like if things had been different.

There are some nights that seem impossible to live through, when it seems as though the night itself is enough to destroy you. That night was like that. And it is true, some part of me did not live through until the morning. Some part of me died in the night. And I can feel it still, I can feel its small dead body, its lifelessness cradled behind my ribs. It is like the hook of a moon. It is a thin sharp sliver of a thing.

Neither of us knew any more what it was that we wanted. And while I tell myself that it is impossible to kill something that had not yet begun, I know that it had, a struggling thing though it was. That is what we were: we were all beginning, and then all end.

We stared at each other. We stared at each other again. Over your shoulder I could see a man and a woman eating together. They were seated at a small table close to the wall. I could see the woman's face, pale, with crimson lipstick, but the man's back was towards me. They were not looking at each other. In fact they were scarcely speaking. She did not appear sad though, or troubled, she just looked enormously bored, bored with the meal, bored with his company, her eyes drooping and vacant. She hardly looked at her food as she ate, nor did she eat as though she were hungry. She was eating the risotto; I knew this because I was eating the same.

We looked at each other again. With the approach of the waiter I looked away. He filled up our water glasses and left. You did not drink yours and so I drank both of them. What do you think you might do with your life now? I asked.

He was not sure. He offered a list of things. He said he thought he might study again, or get a different job, teach maybe.

He asked me the same. I guess I will find some work, I said. Move into the city. Get on with my life, I suppose.

Yes, he replied, that is what people say, isn't it. That is what we say.

We were silent again then. From where I was seated I could see out into the courtyard at the front of the restaurant. There was a white fountain with an angel standing in the centre and pouring water from a vessel. A light shone on it in the darkness and made it glow. I watched it. Another couple came in, tall, dark, elegant twin figures, and were seated to the right of us. The waiter addressed them by name as he seated them and wished them a happy anniversary. I was startled by this, but of course, they must have booked. I imagine the man booked and that when he did, he must have said to the person on the other end of the phone that he and his wife were going out to celebrate.

It was a beautiful restaurant. It was quite delicious food, the dessert especially, a crème brulée, which we shared; we had two spoons and we fed each other. I think it was one of the most beautiful meals I have ever eaten. And in between staring at him and watching my food, I watched the spotlit angel in the courtyard pouring water.

He watched me then. I felt it and for a moment I let him look at me without returning his gaze. I let him think his thoughts and then I looked at him. I looked at him and I knew then that I would never again ask him in quite the same way what it was that he was thinking. And that he need no longer ask me what was on my mind. We were both quite suddenly full of things that we did not and would not know. While all the time we held each other's eyes.

You leaned back in your chair then and the music stopped. It is the mark of a good restaurant that one only notices the music when it ceases. It was quite painful that – suddenly not having any sound between us – between all of us eating there that night. I could feel every person tense with the discomfort that what they were or were not saying to one another would be heard. But the silence ended. The music started again and the conversations around us resumed. It was Spanish music, there were people singing and guitars. It was quite lovely and I found myself listening to it and no longer wanting to force us to speak.

The anniversary couple across from us finished their entrée and began on their mains. The sad couple asked for the bill and prepared to leave, the woman fishing in her handbag for her lipstick. With the aid of a small hand mirror she put it on in front of her husband while they were still seated, no longer needing to hide these things from him, no longer trying to impress him with a sudden and unexpected beauty.

What time is it? you asked. I didn't know. I owned a watch but I never wore it, disliking the feeling of it tight around my wrist, and I had left it accidentally in my bag in the car. Not that time mattered anyhow. But it was something that we asked each other, more out of curiosity concerning how it comes and has come to pass, rather than what time it actually is. We must have been here some time, you said. Yes, I replied, I should think so.

It was the strangest thing, to let go like that. So much so that by the time we came to the end of it, it made so little sense that we should leave each other so completely.

Although it had been my suggestion that we went out to dinner I had forgotten my wallet and so he paid. He asked for the bill, and when the waiter brought it he asked us if we needed a taxi. We must have looked like tourists, young and in love. No, we said, we're fine thanks. We left a small tip, only a dollar or so, and felt a little guilty, thinking that we should have left more, the waiter had been so polite and the food had been good. We had even shared it, as couples do – he asked for a taste of mine and I stopped him from taking a bite himself, instead putting some on my fork and feeding it to him. Here, he said then, offering me his, help yourself. He thought his was too salty and said that I had chosen better.

A waiter brought our coats. There was another couple seated to our left and as we stood to leave the woman looked at me so strangely. I remember it clearly and yet I cannot work it out. It was almost a stunned look, as though she, like us, did not know whether we were in great love or great pain. As though she could see how much we were caught between the two and could remember this feeling herself. I met her gaze as I pulled my coat on. I knew it looked as though I had not slept in weeks. There were grey circles under my eyes and my skin was pale. My lipstick had been chewed off. Maybe she had seen how often we had almost come to tears. I don't know.

Was this how he left his children, the way we then left each other? To love something, to love it and leave it anyway. Because we are selfish and because we do not understand one another. We say we do, we say that we would like to, and we try. But we do not understand. And if we did, if he knew me in that place in which I am a stranger to him, I would resent him. I would come to resent the fact that I had let him in. Despite myself, I never had any intention of handing myself over although that was what I did. We gave ourselves and we took ourselves away. And there we were, preparing for our own death, talking about it as though we might watch it arrive, as though we might wait for it and still remain in one another's company. And who left who? It was impossible to say, although I was the one that moved into the city while he remained where we had been. But that does little to clarify how the end came, who did what to whom, as though we were two, different people. That was not how it was. In the end everything was indistinguishable. Our bodies taking pain and pain and pain until it killed us. It overwhelms me, our capacity to love, our capacity to suffer, how badly we need to feel full even if it is with emptiness. For I was looking for some truth in you and what was it that I found? That we love only to suffer, suffer to love and find things only to lose them again.

We left. The waiter was drinking and playing cards at a table by the kitchen. He nodded at us as we departed and smiled briefly. We said goodbye and went out into the cold, out into the black water of the night. It was freezing outside, the wind was so sharp. We held each other to keep warm and with his free hand he took a cigarette from his pocket, put it to his mouth and tried to light it. I cupped my hand around the flame to keep out the wind and he thanked me.

And later I could still taste him, although he was no longer there. I could taste his smoke at the back of my throat, when, in conversation, he must have exhaled just as I breathed in to speak. When I must have been caught in that moment between breathing, when neither of us was full nor empty, in the passage between the inside and the outside of my body, between a language of thought and a language of speech.

We walked back up the main road to where the car was parked. All the shops were closed and there was nobody about. Only the bottle shop was open and an Italian restaurant. A neon sign above the chemist's flickered. It was cold. We held on to each other because of the cold.

Here, he said, take my jacket.

No, I replied.

Take it.

No.

He took it off and put it over my shoulders anyway. I did not put my arms in. Then we were both freezing.

And I thought, dark harbour me. I thought, steal something from my surface and row out into my dark cold. I would let you go there, I would let you lose yourself to me. Out into the problem that we could not hold.

We reached the car, got in quickly and drove home. We were separating and driving home to spend the night together. Over our meal he had said that it would be better if he left that night. But I had said no. Please stay, I said. I know that I said this even though it was just as much me who was leaving. But he agreed. Why did he agree? Only because I asked him to? Because he didn't want to refuse me, because we had come so often to refuse so many things? I do not know. He did not mean it, for later he changed his mind and he did leave. He said, we have to end this thing, there has to be an end to this. And he was right. Even though we were both crying, and outside it was dark and cold, and I did not want him to go and he did not want to go, but one of us had to and he was the one who had the car.

I cried until I vomited and he came into the bathroom after me. He spoke my name, my full name, as he did. Oh – he said, oh – and wiped my face and helped me up. Wash your hands, he said, and as I did he walked away. He told me these things, but he did not tend to me. He had ceased with this. In fact he was already turning away as he spoke, he was already tired of it all. I could see the shadow of his body on the green tiles. Wash your hands, he said, wash your hands.

And he left not long after that. I could not say goodbye.

He went out into the cold night and I heard him start the car. I heard him reverse out over the gravel and saw the headlights come in through the lounge room windows and swing away as he turned onto the road. Passing the trees. Passing the lake's white pylons.

He phoned the next day. Said he would be away three days so as to give me time to pack my things and leave. I agreed that this was the best way to do things. We did not want to say goodbye again.

So I was leaving.

I told Isabel. I told her that I was moving to the city. We stood at my door. The sun was behind her, shining in my face and through her thin clothes. I didn't know if I should invite her in. I didn't and we were brief. She said she'd keep in touch. I knew she was only saying that and it is true that I have not heard from her since. We didn't touch. I didn't bend forward to kiss her cheek.

I had left things at her house though and in the afternoon she came to return them, some clothes, books that she had never read. It was getting cold and the clouds gathered, grey above the garden, while we stood in the kitchen amongst cardboard boxes and drank cold water from coloured mugs because I had already packed the glasses.

There was a chill in the air with all the doors and windows open, so I folded my arms across my chest for some sort of warmth. But I didn't want her to think I was being defensive. Indeed, there was nothing to defend, there never had been, except for what we each feared or hoped ourselves to be, never sure if the other had seen our secrets.

Boxes full of books dulled the edges of our voices. My boxes of books – cubic square metres thick with paper, although I had hardly read a thing in at least two years.

We did not know, after a while, after a pause that lasted too long, where to look. I stared at the floor as she shifted her weight from one leg to the other, breathing in as though she were about to speak, but said nothing. I looked at the shelves and wondered what I would eat that night; I presumed I would be staying one last night. There were some potatoes in a red plastic bag, and half a bottle of wine corked on the bench. I imagined us then, him and me, not her, cooking and sleeping between boxes, and leaving the house before it knew, as places do, that we were departing.

So, I thought, this is how we love. Turning our eyes away as we try to speak. She said something about missing the company of the dog; she looked to her, patted her, taking the opportunity offered by animals to digress. I told her I would not be taking the dog, that she would have to stay here. So, we said, so. Not knowing how to end the conversation. I'll let you get back to it, she said, as if I had been busy. No, I said, it is all done, but she left anyway.

The next day she did not come over for tea. The sudden apparent separateness between him and me, the intimacy evident in our new difference, made it clear that we were closer than she and I had ever imagined ourselves to be. It was strange in that we knew we could stand each other's absence, Isabel and I, and because of that never had a need to promise to each other that we would be here or be away. It was accepted that we would be both. I accepted it, because, in part, I expected that he would remain, or that I would – with him.

The weather had turned again. Quickly, the cold came quickly. Already I could blow rings with my cold white breath in the mornings. Those last two mornings. I did not speak to Isabel again. Although I saw her come and go from the house.

I couldn't comprehend our silence then, and it is only now, after seeing him walk away, seeing that his thoughts were not with me, that I think I sense something of what it was she felt she had lost, what it was that she suspected we had never really had. My world, she saw, even when I was leaving, remained with him.

If he were to see her now he probably would not remember her by name. He would call her my friend. He would remember the colour of her hair – pale it was, he would say, or he might call it yellow – but I imagine that he would not remember her face.

I saw such yellow today.

It was windy and I was in my hotel room. A woman on her lunch break was walking quickly down the street carrying a bunch of yellow tulips spiked with cutting-grass. From my window it looked as though she was wearing an elaborate headdress, the yellow and the spray of razor green fanning out around her hair as she held it before her. She was in high black shoes with a short skirt and was walking with the wind against her.

She turned her head for a moment. There was a crack in the sidewalk before her and I saw it coming and thought, step over it, step over it, but she didn't see it and fell, the point of her shoe catching in the concrete, and as her arms flew out to save her the flowers spilled everywhere, at least a dozen tulips and the grass, and she, scrambling about on the ground in her short skirt, trying to pick each one up before anyone stood on them.

He never spoke much of the past. When this world finally fails there is always the moon, he had said. It saddened me when I heard this, as though there was no hope left, but he didn't mean it that way. It was that he knew, in some way, that all good things end, and that beyond them, beyond us, are ways of being that are difficult to imagine.

This was the voice I used when I said to him, in his voice, I'm leaving now, as though I too were turning to the moon. I left a message on the answering machine where he was staying. I thought I should tell him so that he knew it was safe to come back. Then I ordered a taxi. If he had been there he would have offered me a lift and I would have tried to refuse. But we did not have to do that again.

I took a cheap flat in a lane off Elizabeth Street. It was a small flat in an old building. Mine was a bare room on the second floor and white, all of it was white, the outside walls, the inside, overlooking the dimmer residue of the city.

There was little furniture. To one side of the bedroom was a wardrobe and a chest of drawers. There was a lamp in one corner and a faded print of a beach scene hanging from a nail on the wall. Beneath this lay a single striped mattress, water-stained and sagging in the middle, a pile of grey woollen blankets folded at the end of it.

The window was open and a venetian blind clanked slowly in the breeze that aired the room of its smell of emptiness – the hollow smell of walls and floors, and not the waxiness of people. I tied the blind so it would not clank and from the window looked down into the laneway and, across from me, to someone's washing hanging from a rope.

I was alone. With winter approaching it was dark well before I was hungry and I did not know what to do with such hours, prior to a desire for food and in the absence of company. I made sure I found things. I made myself read, I fixed the lamp, its cord had been frayed, and found a lounge chair on the pavement which someone had thrown out. I cleaned things. The blind. The floor. Even the walls and the ceiling. I scrubbed down a set of white wooden chairs and a table, both of which I had come across in the street. But eventually, after several nights, I put on my jacket and closed the door behind me.

I took a table in the corner of a restaurant. A couple of men sat outside in coats, drinking and talking. Another man came in, followed by a woman. He had in his hand a small bottle of wine but they were not together. They sat separately. The waiter poured the man a glass as he pulled out the paper from his coat pocket, but he scanned it only briefly before folding it again and looking out the window. He turned and I caught his eye without meaning to. We looked away.

There was a bell above the door which rang each time it opened. Someone else entered. A breeze followed and the man with the paper turned up the collar of his coat. He tried again to read. I understood these constant failing attempts, as he picked up the paper, put it down and picked it up again. I would have liked to tell him that the world would not change so much in a day, that the news was already old. He persisted but it was clear he was not concentrating. Finally he took out a cigarette and lit it. A waiter came up and asked him not to smoke. He appeared confused, as though he always smoked there.

He was still arguing with the waiter when I got up to pay. I had shoved some money into the pocket of my coat, but there was a hole in it and the coins had escaped into the lining. I was two dollars short. I told the waitress that I had the money there somewhere, and bent down, feeling along the hem for coins. She tapped her red polished nails on the bench. She was not smiling. I found a coin and worked it slowly back up to the pocket, pulled it through the hole carefully, as though alive, and held it out only to find it was not two dollars but twenty cents. I could feel myself sweating. I tried to explain – I told her that I didn't live far, that I could bring her the money in the morning. That yes, she was right, although she had said nothing, I really should fix my coat.

He was standing behind me listening. Also waiting to pay. He said something and pushed two dollars across the bench. I wished he hadn't although I was relieved. I wished if he were going to offer money he would at least introduce himself, be slightly familiar. He didn't. I thanked him and left.

The bell above the door rang after me and then again. He asked me my name. I turned around and for a moment considered making one up but none came to mind and instead I paused and stumbled over my own as though it were fake. He held out his hand. My palms sweated, I did not know what to do with strangers. I did not know what to say. Thank you, I offered, taking his hand, for that, motioning towards the restaurant with my head.

No problem, he said.

We stood a moment.

You live around here? he asked, referring to what he had overheard.

Yes. And you?

Yes.

He said he would offer me a lift but he did not have a car. I prefer walking, I said. I'd be happy to walk with you, but – he scuffed his foot against the end of a cigarette. He looked up. Would you like a drink?

The bar he took me to was noisy. We had to lean in close and watch each other's mouth as we spoke. He could smoke there. I did not. He noticed and lifted his chin slightly to the ceiling each time he breathed out, showing the pale ribbing of his throat.

When we left soon after the weather had changed. Clouds cut across the sky and there was a cold wind. We walked close as the wind blew against us and into our mouths. And then it would be still again. On and off, off and on. He asked where my place was and offered to pay for a taxi. Are you sure? I said, uncertain of what to do with chivalry. He pressed one finger to my shoulder and told me to wait, then ran ahead, towards the traffic lights where a taxi had stopped. I watched him run away from me and then I could see that his head was in the window of the car. He lifted it out and waved at me to follow.

Opening the door, he put his hand on my upper back as I bent down and slid in. With the slightest increase of pressure I could say that he pushed me, but he didn't.

We drove off. We got stuck at the next set of lights and the one after. The traffic was bad. I told the driver that where we were would be fine. He was insistent that he take us to the door. No no, I said again, here's fine. We paid and got out. A car behind us sounded its horn as we dodged across the road towards the laneway.

I took him home, all sense of reason at once clear and quite beyond me as we stood at the door, the room seeming even barer in company. The harsh light from the single bulb made him appear sharp and distant, holographic almost – I could see the blue veins through the skin of his hands. I turned off the light, excuse me, I said, but offered no reason. There was then just the neon glow from a street light outside the window, filtering towards us through the branches of a tree.

He lit another cigarette as he leaned against the window, an old fashioned window made of thin glass that opened and closed with a rope pulley. He had his back to it so that he was facing me, but with the brightness of the street behind him I could not make out his features. Outside, rain began falling. I saw it hit the glass, saw the smoke leave his mouth, slowly, and disperse towards the ceiling. Below, on the pavement, I could hear two people arguing. I would come to discover that almost everybody broke up beneath that window, because there was a street light and they could see each other's faces.

He moved towards the fireplace and put his cigarette out on the grate, his knees cracking and his hands sliding over the legs of his pants. I could taste my mouth sour and dry with wine.

I heard, he said, going back to the window, that it's going to rain until Saturday.

Really.

So they say.

Rain.

I went to the window and stood beside him. A woman and a man walked quickly down the lane, the wet top of their umbrella shining under the streetlight. The man was holding her by the waist as they moved with their heads down and the wind against them, the woman turning the umbrella so that it pointed forward like a shield.

She's only in a dress, he said.

Yes.

At the end of the lane they turned the corner and disappeared.

We stood silently before the window. I had nothing to say. I had known the rain. Know it. And it was not his. How could I talk to him about the rain?

I walked away from him then and leaned against the mantelpiece. He came towards me. Put his hand on my back. Through the window a billboard stared at us from the wall of a building.

Loneliness has a smell to it. It was on his hands. I had noticed them – long fingers, soft, no ring, the little finger of his right hand bent by a car door as a child. I had asked this. Injuries. I should have known then.

His body was thinner than she had expected. He had a wide face but a thin body. His skin was soft and he was quiet. Lying on her back, he pulled down her pants, and moved one hand between her legs. She moved away from it, his hand, turned over and moved down his stomach, putting her mouth over him. His hands moved in her hair. She let him enter her, gently at first, while she lay there, listening for the harbour in the dark but could not hear it. Listening for a fog horn but there was none. No, she said, or thought she said, with his breath in her face, his mouth moving towards her ear. She did not want him, but the human voice has a fashion of failing in such conditions. He was supposed to be for her all these independent and newfound things – she had thought it would be – new and independent – but it was instead, or rather it became, a sort of clambering over rough fields with him coming up behind her. She moved towards the edge. He pulled her back. She moved towards the edge again. It was a normal motion, the lovemaking that they had, with her asking herself if this is the way by which we take each other, too desperately, him hanging onto her neck like a dog. It is an odd manner we have sometimes, she thought, her thought remaining – as it can when the body is propelled into urgency – entirely lucid, that we attack someone more and more savagely when we want them to come towards us. When we are hungry, we deprive ourselves; when we approach happiness, we speak of it in contrast to our sorrow. She did not think herself perverted as he turned her over so that she faced him with her back. And with her face pushed against the pillow she cried. He did not notice, but finished, making a sound she had not heard from a man before, as though he were choking, gagging on the body that had just been consumed.

She saw a boy once, in summer, standing at the edge of the ocean. As a wave came forward the boy leaned back then flung himself towards the water. It was as though he were being flayed, the heaving of a body in response to a force like pain. His arms and chest and waist would hurl themselves towards the wave, and then stop short, letting the wave attack him but never entering it. He threw himself again, and stopped, again, and stopped. As though nearing flight, and then refusing it. Giving himself to the violence of a thing but never giving himself away.

He should have cried, she thought, for some reason, for some reason he should have cried. In the depths of pleasure he should have touched his pain. But he didn't. He finished and collapsed on top of her.

Afterwards he couldn't find his jacket. It's in the kitchen, she said.

Thanks. Coins rattled in the pocket as he pulled it on, slowly, one arm then the other. The brass buttons clicking together as he shrugged it over his shoulders. She stood near the door, watching his preparations, as he took some money out, counted it, put it back. She moved aside so he could leave, and pausing, he kissed her on the cheek. He left and she closed the door behind him.

I had thought that it would be easy. To have had a red light and then a green. I had not planned what my life then would be like. We simply thought our lives would be new: light, free even. They should have just been new, we said.

I returned to the restaurant the following night. I ate a little, I asked for water. I glanced at the menu while I watched the door and told the waitress I was waiting for a friend.

He didn't return. I didn't expect him to. It was a quiet night, I watched the woman at the bar spend her evening drying beer glasses. If he had turned up I don't know what we would have said. Still, each time the bell above the door rang I flinched a little, looked up. The entrance to the restaurant was a small alcove, darker than the street outside lit by lamplight, so that it was only possible to see the mass of the person entering but nothing more. So with each man I squinted, hoped, but it was not him.

It was not either of them.

The city has closed up its colours in the rain. The flower stalls and the fruit stalls which spread their goods over the pavement have gone. I did not expect this. When I thought of the city and imagined arriving in it I had envisaged, always, the random explosions of fruit and flowers on the roadside.

Instead the streets are grey. The only brightnesses are the round yellow signs for the bus stops and the coloured displays in shop windows. The occasional umbrella. Blue and green. Red and yellow. A woman in sandals with white feet.

I went walking through the city the day after he had not returned to the restaurant. It was afternoon, coming into evening, and the rain had cleared. It was cold though and windy. I took the stairs from my room and as I walked down two men came up. They were speaking in French and their voices echoed in the stairwell, burbled. They made, I thought, the sound of memories; that of two people trying to speak to each other underwater.

When anything dies we wish we had done more. Wish that we had talked more, cared more, feared less. Especially when you have known for some time that the thing is leaving, known that you have had the chance to do the more that later you regret not having done. And, strangely, it seems exactly that which prevents the care: the fear we have of things leaving. One is afraid of what to do with something so close to disappearance, so close to a world unknown. We are so afraid of what we do not understand but what is not itself fearful.

Were I to offer these words to you now and say, this is for you, it would be because of the above. For it is much easier to thank someone, care for someone, dedicate something to them when they have gone, when they are held in the vessel of the past which lets only an unequal kind of peace be achieved, a peace that belongs to one self and never two, encompassing, alone, what together, was not, or could not, be accomplished.

I tell myself that it is all good, and all true, and must mean something, must account for something, these intentions, these well-wishings that we hold with regard to the figures of our past. And it does, I think. And at the same time it does not. Because I did not do what I did not do, the things I wish I had done, even though I am doing this. Although I know, however much I might once have argued against this, that one cannot do everything. One cannot. However much I might try. How we all try. It can only come down to the fact now that we did not do what we did not do, and that now, as then, I will do what I can. And we could only ever do what we could. He had said this.

I wonder now if people are not in fact filled with secrets the way I used to think they were. The way we used to lie together in the night while you asked me things and I told you what no one else knew. The pleasure of being able to confide. And for you I'd do the same, ask you questions, listen to you speak. Then there were endless discoveries, every small thing was something to be known.

I do not believe in this any more. I do not believe in secrets and their intimacy. We did not need to tell of them. For so much of what you told me I could have guessed. And even that would not have made a difference. I either loved you or I did not. I either knew everything from the very start or I would always know nothing. An image comes to mind – of corsets and the hoops that women used to wear under skirts, this discrete skeleton on top of a body on top of bones. We had not failed. Instead we had been forced to go where no one should.

My mother asked when she came one morning if I was writing this down. No, I said, why? You should keep a diary of it, to remember. Write it down, she said. Write what, where? That room, that tired body. It is impossible to forget.

I did try though. I sat at my desk the next morning with a pen and paper. I wrote the date: November twenty-eight. I do not know why I wrote that date, I do not think it was the date the day belonged to. I did not know such things any more. Then I began. I wrote something about my body. What I thought it felt like, but it was not that and eventually I stopped.

This afternoon I walked across the city, towards the harbour, and up towards the park and the pool, where, even in winter, there were people swimming. In the park was a fountain – I remembered this fountain, shooting up into the air, the wind blowing the jet of water across the grass. On the pond ducks pulled their necks down into their feathers.

As I made my way back toward the hotel I passed a funeral. I couldn't see any people, there was just a black car outside a church. There were flowers wrapped in paper in the back, yellow flowers, and an old man, the driver of the car, standing on the steps shuffling to keep out the cold. The sun had gone behind the buildings by then and the street was in shadow. I could hear an organ playing inside the church. There was no one singing. Outside, on the pavement a plastic lunch wrapper blew about while at the bus stop a woman sat feeding her baby.

On the ground, fallen leaves were tossed by my feet as I walked quickly to keep out the cold, and pigeons, there were pigeons, and two boys chasing them across my path, causing the birds to scatter, switch and swing in another direction. I moved away from the sudden spiral of birds and leaves and the children, and as the birds fled from the pavement they flew so close I could feel them, almost sense the soft thud of a bird against me. They scalloped the air into my ears as the two boys crashed into me, pelting bread crusts at the pigeons in the hope that they would stop.

It occurred to me at first to punish him by not speaking to him. But punish him for what – for all the pain? As if it were not his too. It did not occur to me that he might do the same. And so now we are silent, keeping ourselves as though we could be secrets.

I wonder what I would have done had I not come across him in the city this last time. How I might have hoped differently, how I might have kept searching and thinking, that, unfairly, I had not been given another chance, when really we were given two. For I think of that place now, our place, in the mountains, as I have always thought of it – the way one considers, with fondness and pain, an absent person. I wonder what colour it is, how cold, if there are clouds. And I see the cliffs, thinking of those welts where the rock has come away from itself. Grey at first then red beneath the surface. And I wonder who has been there since me and how they might have changed it and that I might not ever know it like I did, at first, before I had a history there, before I had left and not returned, making belonging like erosion – the way water works itself through rock and makes its moving place there.

I should write this down, I said to you, at the end of it. No one would believe it, you said. I do not have to tell the truth, I replied.

And so I tell this story, which is true to the extent that I knew you, although if I told it to you I have no doubt that you would say it is wrong, that this was not the way it was. And you would be right. I have lied. But it is only common sense that time changes the truth of everything, and perhaps it is more that you often found it difficult to believe what I said, for it is almost impossible to understand another's pain or illness if it has not been your own, and even if it has, so often it leaves no trace of itself and is quickly and deliberately forgotten.

You asked me one afternoon, when we were drinking, if what I was writing about was you. No, I said. You seemed neither relieved nor disappointed. You seemed like nothing. So often you seemed like nothing, your face fallen in the bright sunlight by the water. And your hair. There was sunlight in your hair, making it dark brown and not black at all.

I turned to you and said that if I left you now, maybe it would be.

It was a hot day. The white umbrellas propped up over the tables were glaring in the sunlight and the ends of the palm leaves had turned brown in the heat.

In a shop across the road two women were trying on hats. They were friends, one supervising the hat choice of the other. The first one, the shorter of the two, tried on a straw hat with a red band. She pushed it down on her hair. Red was not her colour, her friend seemed to suggest. She tried green.

There was a siren in the distance. Every time we tried to speak there seemed to be a siren in the distance and one of us would say, listen, there is a siren, and we would listen instead of speaking. Even as I walked back to the hotel along Broadway after seeing you that day there was a siren. It was a fire engine. As it passed a man walked by. He was talking on his phone. The woman at the other end, I'm sure it was a woman for he called her baby, must have heard the siren and commented on it, must have asked what was happening, for I heard the man say to her, that's right baby, I'm always in the middle of a fire.

I have seen him.

It was an accident. For both of us it was an accident. I saw him because the rain came again and because it was Friday when all along I had been thinking that it was Saturday and that tomorrow would be Sunday and I would be gone. But I was mistaken, for it was Friday, and so of course he was there and I should have considered this, having considered it in such detail every other day, for I had decided by then that I would not see him again, that I would no longer allow myself to look out for him on the street and should have realised that it was Friday and not Saturday seeing that everyone was still dressed for business and occupying business hours, and yet there I was, living one day ahead of myself.

I had gone into the bar I knew he used to go to; it was pouring by then and my umbrella had finally given up in the wind, the black cloth ripping from the spokes so that I could only abandon it. This made me late, late arriving and late leaving, late because of the rain, because of the wine, because I still hoped that I would see him, although I had decided that I would not. As I left my table, I turned my head to look down the corridor to where the bar was. He was there. I knew it was him. I knew it was him and he knew it was me. He was standing at the bar facing the street, and me, and in conversation with another woman. She had her back to me, facing him. She was talking. I saw his face follow me. I saw his face follow me while mine hung itself on him while all the while, all the while, my body moved me away. I stared hard, I could not see the details of his face, my eyes failing me as they have come to fail me over time, unable to read the time on a clock or the signs outside shopping centres, and so although I knew it was him I could not make out all of his face, but just the shape of it – his white skin, shirt, his dark hair and suit as I knew him.

I stared, hours pressed into the briefest moment of surprise. I could not take my head away from him and neither could I speak and all the while, all the while, although it was only a matter of metres – a matter of seconds – my body continued to move me away from him. I imagine that he would not at first have recognised me, or perhaps would have immediately, and for a moment would not have wished to believe what he saw, as I had wished, each of us recognising the other far too well.

I was not walking away from you. Please, do not think I was walking away from you. You were standing still and I happened to be the one moving. What else could I do. What else could we have done, with you standing still and me moving. I could only keep walking, and I walked hard, and walked out into the rain, where the sound of the traffic took everything away, although I hoped, I hoped, that I would hear him come running up behind me. Once he would have done that.

No. I lie. He had never done that. He never would, not if I had been the one to walk away. He was always so careful not to do anything that might contravene my wishes. He saw me go and could have only thought that that was what I wanted.

Printed in Great Britain
by Amazon

27677135R00121